A BULLET WAS THE ANSWER

The next moment a husky shadow separated from a tent on the left and strode into the middle of the street. Smirking, Rowdy Joe Guthrie adopted a wide stance. His pistol was in its scabbard, his arms loose at his sides. He did not say anything until Fargo reined up. "This is as far as you go, mister. Climb down."

Fargo had his revolver out. He could have shot Guthrie before the killer touched his six-shooter, but he slid off and twirled his own into its holster.

"Who is he?" Fargo asked. "Who's the hombre who set this whole thing up?"

"Find out for yourself," Rowdy Joe said, his hand dropping to his pistol even as he spoke.

Only a greenhorn would fall for the ruse. And Fargo was no greenhorn. Their shots were a split second apart, but his blasted first. . . .

THE
TRAILSMAN
#205

MOUNTAIN
MANKILLERS

by

Jon Sharpe

A SIGNET BOOK

SIGNET
Published by the Penguin Group
Penguin Putnam Inc., 375 Hudson Street
New York, New York 10014, U.S.A.
Penguin Books Ltd, 27 Wrights Lane,
London W8 5TZ, England
Penguin Books Australia Ltd,
Ringwood, Victoria, Australia
Penguin Books Canada Ltd, 10 Alcorn Avenue,
Toronto, Ontario, Canada M4V 3B2
Penguin Books (N.Z.) Ltd, 182–190 Wairau Road,
Auckland 10, New Zealand

Penguin Books Ltd, Registered Offices:
Harmondsworth, Middlesex, England

First published by Signet, an imprint of Dutton NAL,
a member of Penguin Putnam Inc.

First Printing, December, 1998
10 9 8 7 6 5 4 3 2 1

The first chapter of this book originally appeared in
The Leavenworth Express Company,
the two hundred fourth volume in this series

 REGISTERED TRADEMARK—MARCA REGISTRADA

Printed in the United States of America

The Trailsman

Beginnings . . . they bend the tree and they mark the man. Skye Fargo was born when he was eighteen. Terror was his midwife, vengeance his first cry. Killing spawned Skye Fargo, ruthless, cold-blooded murder. Out of the acrid smoke of gunpowder still hanging in the air, he rose, cried out a promise never forgotten.

The Trailsman they began to call him all across the West: searcher, scout, hunter, the man who could see where others only looked, his skills for hire but not his soul, the man who lived each day to the fullest, yet trailed each tomorrow. Skye Fargo, the Trailsman, and the seeker who could take the wildness of a land and the wanting of a woman and make them his own.

*1861—the mile-high Rockies, where a fiery mix
of gold and greed proved to be more explosive
than a keg of black powder . . .*

1

The place had an air of danger about it, like a snake den swarming with rattlers. Or a pool of quicksand waiting to suck in unwary victims.

The Trailsman stared at the grungy mining camp from atop a high ridge and did not like what he saw. He could not say why. The camp was no different from countless others that had sprung up since word leaked of gold in the Rockies. Word of the fortunes to be made, if a person were lucky enough. If they survived the long trek West, the hostiles and the bandits, the heat and the storms, the drought and widespread disease. And if, by some miracle, they were one of the rare few to actually stumble on a rich vein.

Most of those who came wound up dirt poor, or dead. Yet that had not stopped thousands from flocking to the mile-high mountains, where many of the stark peaks were crowned year-round with glistening mantles of snow. Gold fever was hard to shake, and more contagious than the measles. Once a man was infected, he might desert his friends, his kin, even his own wife and children, and set off with a crazed gleam in his eyes in search of his personal El Dorado.

Skye Fargo wanted no part of it. He had never been rich and had no real hankering to be. If it happened, it happened. Fine. But he was not about to go mad with gold lust, as so many had. His treasure was the wilderness itself. His treasure, and his home. Sparkling stars were the roof over his head at night, his bed always a cushion of soft grass.

Yes, there were perils, but no life was risk-free. And having to deal daily with savage beasts and even more savage men had unforeseen benefits. For one thing, it had honed his senses to a razor's edge. He could see a hawk soar a mile off, could hear the whisper of a butterfly's wings. He had few rivals when it came to tracking. And somehow he had acquired a sort of special intuition, a feeling that came over him whenever unseen danger loomed.

Such as now. Fargo's piercing lake-blue eyes narrowed as he studied the mining camp. There were the usual collection of grimy tents and rickety shacks. Plus a few buildings substantial enough to withstand a strong Chinook. Few people were abroad but it was early yet, only the middle of the afternoon. Most were off along Dew Creek or its tributaries, working their claims. Come nightfall, the gold-crazed legion would return and turn the quiet camp into a raging hell.

Fargo intended to be long gone by then. He was inclined to give the camp a wide berth but he was in need of a few supplies. With a toss of his head he shook off the feeling of unease and clucked to the Ovaro. He held to a walk as he descended, his right hand on his thigh close to his Colt. His hat brim was pulled low against the stiff breeze that stirred the whangs on his buckskins.

A crudely painted sign identified the camp. DEW CLAW, Fargo read. He had never heard of it, but that was not unusual. Mining camps had shorter life spans than most moths. They were here today, gone tomorrow. Or as soon as the latest strike played out. Originally, Dew Claw had a population of 210. But someone had crossed that out and written 794 below. Then the 794 had been crossed off, and a new figure, 1431, added. But that last number no longer applied, either. A knife had carved an X over it. And at the bottom of the sign, in bold red letters, had been scrawled: "Who the hell cares?" Fargo could not help but grin.

A few weary horses were tied to makeshift hitch rails. Dirty men in dirtier clothes were everywhere. The street—if it could be dignified by such a grand term—was inches thick in clinging mud. The whole camp was as glum as the cloudy sky overhead.

Several dandies in store-bought clothes stood out like proverbial sore thumbs. Fargo had seen their kind before. Human vultures. Those who flocked to wherever gold was found to prey on those who found it. Those who lined their pockets with the dust and nuggets that rightfully belonged to others. Storekeepers who marked up the cost of goods five hundred percent. Gamblers who had more cards up their sleeves than in their decks. Footpads who would as soon knife a man in the ribs as look at him.

Fargo drew the gaze of everyone he passed. Big and broad-shouldered, he was a tawny panther among half-starved wolves. Some of the stares were merely curious. Others were unfriendly. A large, scruffy man in a bulky coat glanced his way, looked off, then glanced at him again, a hint of recognition dawning.

An empty rail beckoned. Fargo drew rein and started to ease his right foot from the stirrup.

"You can't hitch your animal there, mister."

At the corner of a ramshackle building stood a girl of ten or twelve, all freckles and teeth. Her clothes had been patched up so many times, they appeared as if they had been made from a quilt. Fargo returned her warm smile, then nodded. "This one reserved, is it?" He said it in jest. No one had the right to reserve a hitch rail. First come, first served, was always the general rule.

"Yes, sir," the sprout answered. "Rowdy Joe and his bunch have staked a claim on it. No one else is to tie up here, ever." Dipping a hand into a frayed pocket, she proudly flourished a coin. "He pays me to tell folks to keep away."

The hitch rail was in front of a seedy establishment with the appropriate name of the TIMBERLINE SALOON. Bear hide flaps covered the windows and the solid wood door was closed. It probably would not be open for business for another couple of hours yet. Fargo shrugged and started to dismount. Whoever had the gall to claim the hitch rail would

11

likely not show up until then. So he had plenty of time to buy the supplies he needed and be on his way.

"Hold on!" the girl declared in alarm. "Didn't you hear me? Rowdy Joe won't take it kindly. Buck him and he'll pound you to a pulp, for certain sure. Honest. I've seen him do it to other folks."

"He won't do it to me," Fargo said matter-of-factly while looping the stallion's reins around the pole. Stretching, he scanned the street. A sizeable tent farther down advertised itself as the DEW CLAW MERCANTILE. Fishing fingers into his own pocket, he found an even bigger coin. "Here."

The girl caught it in midair, gaped a moment, then bit it as if to prove it was real. "Golly, mister. A silver dollar. Who do you want me to shoot?"

Fargo chuckled and hooked his thumbs into his gunbelt. "I want you to watch my horse for me. If anyone lays a hand on him or tries to move him, you're to fetch me right away. I'll be in the general store."

"I'll guard him with my life." She beamed. "I'm Amanda, but most people hereabouts call me Mandy. Maybe you'd like to come over to our claim later and meet my sisters? They're both powerful in need of a handsome feller like you."

"Is that a fact?" Fargo responded, wondering if she meant what he thought she meant. Mining camps attracted fallen doves in droves. Having dallied with more than his share, he was always willing to enjoy their company. But not this time. He had to be in Denver in three days on business.

"Yep, it is," Mandy answered. "They're both getting long in the tooth. Why, Nina is pretty near twenty-two! If she doesn't marry soon, she's afeared she'll end her days a lonely old spinster."

Again Fargo chuckled. "Twenty-two is ancient, all right. But I'm not on the hunt for a wife right now. Tell your sisters not to fret. Sooner or later the right man will come along."

"That's what Pa always said," Mandy replied, her features clouding. "Before we lost him."

"Your father died?"

"Yes, sir. Leastwise, we think he did. No one ever found his body. Just blood." Her voice broke and her lower lip quivered. "Happened a fortnight ago. Some say a grizzly was to blame. Others say it was Injuns. My sisters think it was—" Mandy stopped, her gaze drifting past him, her eyes widening in sudden fright.

Fargo turned.

Three men approached. Two had the unmistakable stamp of guns for hire. But the third was a strutting peacock dressed in the finest shirt, pants, and shoes money could buy. In his left hand he twirled a polished cane. To everyone he passed, he nodded, as might royalty to peasants. When he spied the Ovaro, he broke stride. His gaze strayed to Fargo and he smirked. "Well, well. What have we here, Mandy? Someone who wouldn't listen? Didn't you tell him about Rowdy Joe?"

Fargo took an instant dislike to the man. "Ask me, not her," he declared gruffly.

One of the gunmen, a scarecrow whose clawed fingers were hooked to draw, took a step forward but was halted by the peacock's outstretched arm.

"Fair enough, friend. I'm Luke Olinger. I own the Timberline." He said it in the same high-and-mighty fashion the Queen of England might say, "I own the Crown Jewels."

"Good for you."

Olinger's smirk evaporated. Resting the cane on his shoulder, he studied Fargo closely. "You're new here, so I'll make allowances. There are a few facts you should learn. First, I pretty much run Dew Claw. Rile me and you'll regret it. Second, Rowdy Joe is a business associate. As much as I despise him, he's not the kind of man to trifle with. So move your horse while you still can."

Fargo never liked being told what to do. Since he had been knee-high to a buffalo calf, he had resented it. His life was his own, to live as he saw fit. Yet another reason he would never settle back East. He enjoyed his freedom too much to ever let politicians, or anyone else, ride roughshod over him. "The pinto stays put."

The scarecrow gun shark was poised to slap leather. "Just say the word, Mr. Olinger, and I'll move that damn critter. And teach this hombre a lesson, besides."

Olinger was either uncommonly smart or cautious by nature. "Sheathe your claws, Horner. We'll let Rowdy Joe deal with this upstart." The smirk returned and Olinger twirled his cane. "I must thank you in advance, friend, for the entertainment you will shortly provide. The days are so dull in this flea-ridden pit. I much prefer the excitement and gaiety of St. Louis."

Fargo did not care what the dandy liked. "I'm not your friend." Pivoting, he stalked off, as angry at himself as he was at Olinger and Horner. His temper had gotten the better of him. It would have been a simple matter to tie the stallion to another hitch rail. Was his pride so important he was willing to shed blood over a trifle? The answer was Yes! For once a man started backing down, it became a habit. Before he knew it, he was slinking around like a whipped cur, his tail always between his legs. Fargo would be damned if he would ever let that happen to him.

The mercantile was quiet. A couple of middle-aged women were paging through a thick catalog, daydreaming of luxuries they would never own. Behind the counter stood a gray-haired man with spectacles perched on the end of his nose. He looked up from the ledger he was writing in. "Can I help you?"

Fargo's order was a short one. Coffee, ammunition for his Colt and the Henry, and enough jerky to last until Denver. While waiting, he examined a fancy saddle on a rack. The sign said it was a new three-quarter rig. Recently he had seen its like down El Paso way.

Saddles always interested him. His was one of the best. It had to be. He spent more time on horseback than most men, so his rig had to be comfortable as well as practical. Which was why he'd had his custom-made. Like a Texas rig, it sported two cinches. The tree was slightly longer than most, the cantle slightly wider. The apple was higher and flat-topped for ease in wrapping a rope. And where most riders were content to make do with short skirts, he had asked for a full-square skirt under the tree to reduce wear and chaffing on the Ovaro.

The front flap parted. Fargo shifted, alert for trouble, but it was only a young woman. A lovely young woman with luxurious auburn hair, vivid green eyes, and features as fine as any ever chiseled by the best sculptors who ever lived. Her seedy shirt and pants did not detract in the least from her beauty, nor from the vitality she radiated. Chin high, she marched to the counter and smacked a hand down hard. "Lester Cavendar! What's this Ella tells me about our credit being no good?"

The man with the spectacles was on a ladder, removing a can of Arbuckle's from a shelf. Nervously licking his thin lips, he mustered a smile. "Now, now, Nina. Don't you start in on me. Can I help it if your family has run up such a high bill?"

"Who are you trying to kid?" Nina retorted. "Our bill isn't half as large as some. You've cut us off because you were told to. Fess up."

Lester tried to be stern but it was like a kitten trying to act fierce. It just couldn't be done. "See here. I own this store, not anyone else. I can do as I see fit. And I say that unless you pay your outstanding debts, I can't grant you any more credit." He sniffed in disdain. "This is a business, woman. Not a charity. You would do well to remember that."

"Is that so?" Placing both hands flat, Nina swung lithely over the counter, then gripped the ladder. "Now *you* see here. How do you expect my sisters and me to get by? Want us to put on dresses and prance around in saloons?"

"How you make your living is not my concern," Lester said testily. "And I'll thank you to move so I can get down."

But Nina did not budge. Instead, she gave the ladder a little shake. Just enough to cause Lester to shriek and grab hold of a shelf for support. "We need vittles, consarn it. Some dried beans will do. And flour, and butter if you have any."

"What? No bacon? Or maybe you want me to throw in a side of beef for free?" Cavendar's sarcasm was thick enough to cut with a knife. "You're not getting a thing, and that's final."

"I'm not leaving without it," Nina insisted. She shook the ladder again, violently this time. Lester squawked and clung on for dear life, nearly dropping the coffee. "If it were only Ella and me, I wouldn't make a fuss. But we have Mandy to think of. Do you want her to starve to death just because you don't have any backbone?"

Fargo's interest perked. Mandy was the girl by the saloon. So Nina must be one of her sisters. He moved toward the counter.

Lester had more spine than Fargo had figured. Although scared silly, he glared and snapped, "Your family owes twenty-seven dollars and sixty cents. Until that is paid, my hands are tied. If I were to go easy on you, others would expect the same treatment. Why, I'd be bankrupt in no time."

"Have a heart," Nina pleaded. "You know how rough it's been for us since our pa died. But we're still working the claim. We'll be able to pay you off in a couple of weeks."

"When you do, I will gladly sit down and discuss reopening your account. Until then, try rabbit stew. I hear tell there are plenty in the woods."

Nina's cheeks flushed scarlet. "I bet you shed your skin once a month, like a snake! Come down from there so I can scratch your eyes out."

"You wouldn't dare!"

Any fool could see that she would. Fargo cleared his throat and announced, "If the lady has no objections, I'll pay her bill."

Both the beauty and the proprietor were momentarily

flabbergasted. Lester's mouth moved like that of a fish out of water. It was a full five seconds before he found his voice. "What? Who are you? What business is this of yours? You can't settle their account."

Fargo's temper surged anew. What was it about the business owners in Dew Claw, he wondered, that made them think they had the God-given right to boss others around? "It's up to the lady, not you." Nina was inspecting him as if he had just dropped out of the sky. Touching his hat brim, he said, "I couldn't help but overhear. For your sister's sake, let me help you."

"You know Ella?"

"No. Mandy."

Amazement and something else flitted across Nina's face. She flushed again, though not from anger. "I appreciate the kindness, mister. I truly do. But we don't take handouts. We're poor but we don't impose on others. Our pa always told us that we shouldn't be beholden to anyone. So we'll have to decline. Sorry."

"There are no strings attached," Fargo assured her. "If you want, repay me when you and your sisters are back on your feet. Send the money care of the sutler's at Fort Laramie. He's a friend of mine."

"We just couldn't," Nina said, but she was plainly tempted.

"I didn't see one rabbit on the way in," Fargo mentioned. "And I'd hate for Mandy to go hungry because you're too stubborn for your own good."

Nina pursed her mouth. A mouth, Fargo noted, shaped like a ripe strawberry. Her homespun shirt swelled nicely in front, while her thighs were as exquisitely shaped as any he had ever seen. "Are you sure you have the money to spare?" she asked.

Fargo nodded. Just barely. Subtracting the cost of his own provisions, he'd have about two bucks left to his name. Not much, but when he arrived in Denver he was due to collect a couple of hundred. He made a show of counting out the twenty-seven dollars and sixty cents.

Lester had descended. Anyone could tell part of him did not want to take the money and part of him did. Greed won. Scooping it up, he fondled it as a man might a lover. "Consider the sisters all paid up."

"You'll extend them a new line of credit," Fargo said.

The merchant looked at him and opened his mouth as if to object. But something he saw in Fargo's expression changed his mind. "Whatever you say, stranger. I reckon I'm just a generous soul."

"In a pig's eye," Nina muttered. Her green eyes fixed on her tall benefactor and for a fleeting instant betrayed deep gratitude. "I can't thank you enough. We haven't had a decent meal in days. All the money we had disappeared when our pa did. Since then we've been living hand to mouth."

"Glad I can help."

Lester did not know when to leave well enough alone. Snickering, he leaned on an elbow and quipped, "What are you, mister? A Good Samaritan? Or were you hoping to get in this uppity filly's britches?"

Fargo's right hand shot out. His fingers clamped on the owner's throat, clamped tight, and squeezed. Lester grabbed his wrist and pulled and pushed. But the man had the strength of a day-old infant. Fargo shook him as a lynx might shake a rodent. "Not all jackasses have four legs, Cavendar. Savvy?"

Terror-stricken, the proprietor whined.

"I'll be back this way one day. I'd hate to hear that you've mistreated Nina or her sisters. If you agree to behave yourself, blink twice."

Sputtering and wheezing, Lester frantically fluttered his eyelids eight or nine times.

Still squeezing, Fargo smiled at the beauty. "See? Most people will be as polite as can be if you only take the time to explain things to them." He shoved, slamming Cavendar against the shelves with such force they swayed and threatened to topple. "Now, if you'll excuse me, ma'am. I have a lot of hard riding to do before nightfall." Collecting his supplies, Fargo plunked payment down and departed.

Lester never uttered another peep. Doubled over, beet red, he sucked in air like a bellows gone amok. If looks could kill, though, he'd have shriveled Fargo down to the size of an ant just to squish him underfoot.

"Wait, mister!"

Fargo was almost out through the flap. He'd had a bellyful of Dew Claw. It was a hell hole, a festering den of sidewinders and polecats, just like dozens of others he had come across in his travels. Anyone who stayed there was asking for grief. The sooner he was shed of the place, the happier he would be.

"You never told me your handle."

"Skye Fargo." Assuming that was the end of it, he left. He should have known better. She tagged along, chattering like an excited chipmunk.

"Can I call you Skye? I wish you weren't in such an all-fired hurry to leave. Ella and I would be right pleased if you'd come have supper with us. She's a wonderful cook. Her biscuits will melt in your mouth. And her coffee is the best this side of the Mississippi. Pa said so himself many a time."

"Mandy told me he disappeared. Have any idea of what happened to him?"

"You bet I do!" Nina was going to say more but a commotion up the street gave her pause.

A small crowd had gathered in front of the Timberline Saloon. Four men on horseback were also there, close to the hitch rail. A high-pitched voice cried out and was greeted by harsh laughter. Fargo quickened his pace, his gut balling into a knot. He had a fair inkling of what he would find, and shouldering through the spectators, he learned his hunch was right. Mandy had hold of the Ovaro's reins and was trying to keep a husky bull of a man from seizing them. She was scared but trying not to show it.

"Please, Mr. Guthrie! A man paid me to watch over this animal!"

The human bull made a grab at her but Mandy skipped aside, provoking more mirth. Hemmed in as she was, she could not go more than a few feet in any direction. Adding to the poor girl's woes, the Ovaro nickered and bobbed its head, nearly jerking her off balance.

"Try harder, Rowdy Joe!" an onlooker hollered.

"Maybe you should pick on someone smaller," hooted another. "This one is a regular wildcat!"

"She's more than you can handle!" chimed in a third.

Rowdy Joe Guthrie was not amused. His head was as broad as a longhorn's, his forehead as high, and slanted. He had oversized ears that resembled shorn horns, ears his wide-brimmed brown hat could not quite hide. An ill-fitting brown shirt covered his barrel chest. His pants were black. Brawny, calloused hands opened and clenched in irritation as he took a short step and bellowed. "Enough of your shenanigans, girl! Give me the reins and I'll forget how you've bucked me."

Mandy was on the verge of tears. "Please! I don't want to make you mad! But I can't let you beat him anymore!"

That was when Fargo saw the cottonwood switch in Rowdy Joe's left hand and the welt on the pinto's neck. He shook from head to toe, as if cold, but what he felt was fiery inner heat. A red haze seemed to shroud the whole world. Dimly, he was conscious of turning, of shoving the coffee and the ammunition and the jerky into startled Nina's arms. Then his legs were moving of their own accord. His left hand fell on Rowdy Joe's shoulder and spun Guthrie around. His right hand, balled into an iron fist, swept up in a vicious arc, his knuckles smashing full into the bigger man's jaw.

The blow would have felled a lesser foe. Teeth crunched, scarlet drops spattered every which way, and Rowdy Joe tottered back against the hitch rail. The cottonwood switch dropped but Joe did not. Stunned silence gripped the crowd as he snorted, spat blood, then glowered at the Trailsman.

Mandy whooped for joy. "You're back! Thank goodness! I didn't know how much longer I could hold him off!"

Rowdy Joe Guthrie straightened. "So this is your cayuse, is it?"

In the doorway of the saloon someone chortled. Luke Olinger stepped from the shadows, leaned on the jamb, and tapped the wood with the ivory knob on the end of his cane. "Your brilliance never fails to astound me, Joseph. I'm dying to know whether you can count to twelve without taking off your boots." The dandy jabbed the cane in Fargo's direction. "Who else would he be? There isn't another living soul in all of Dew Claw with enough grit to stand up to you."

"Don't use that tone on me," Rowdy Joe warned. "Not unless you want your teeth kicked down your throat."

Luke shook his head and sighed. "Typical. You threaten me, when the curly wolf in front of you is the one you should be venting your spleen on. Or could it be that you're afraid of him?"

"I'm not afraid of anyone or anything!" Rowdy Joe declared. And with that, he lowered his head, extended both arms, and charged Fargo.

2

Rowdy Joe Guthrie did not rely on skill to win a fight. He relied on sheer brute force. Well over six feet tall, weighing upward of two hundred and forty pounds, and packed with solid sinew, his size and bulk were enough to overwhelm most opponents. No doubt Guthrie had won many a saloon brawl and stomped many an enemy under his heel. But brute-force could not win every fight. It had its limits. As the bruiser was about to learn.

Skye Fargo coiled on the balls of his feet as Rowdy Joe charged. He heard Mandy scream, heard Nina call his name. Then he shut them from his mind. Guthrie's great paws were almost within reach when he suddenly ducked and pivoted, thrusting his left leg out as he did.

Rowdy Joe, hurtling headlong, could not stop. Slammed across the shins, he pitched forward. But as he fell, he snagged Fargo's sleeve. Fargo tried to wrench free but Rowdy Joe's fingers dug into his flesh like the jaws on a beaver trap.

"Got you!" Guthrie gloated, yanking.

Fargo was bodily heaved onto his side, next to the larger man. Joe pushed onto his knees, cocked an arm, and swung. He was fast for one his size but not fast enough. The punch grazed Fargo's temple as he rolled backward. Both of them were on their feet in a twinkling, Rowdy Joe smiling smugly, confident in his power. "I'm going to break you, one bone at a time," he vowed.

Fargo said nothing. To talk during a fight was foolish. It

distracted a fighter, made him vulnerable. Raising both fists in a boxing posture, he waited for Guthrie to come at him again. He did not wait long. Rowdy Joe was too impatient to stand back and take his measure, as any smart brawler would.

Roaring lustily, the ruffian hurled himself forward. His arms were outflung, just like before. Triumph lit his features, triumph that changed to chagrin when he swept his arms in a bear hug only to have the one he intended to crush drop below them and skip to the right, out of harm's way. Baffled, he rotated.

"Hold still, damn you!"

Only an idiot would do any such thing, and no one had ever accused Fargo of having rocks between his ears. Braced and ready, he flicked both fists, catching Guthrie on the jaw and the cheek.

The blows rocked Rowdy Joe. Blinking, he touched his chin, then growled like a cornered wolverine and sprang. Fargo backpedaled, the crowd parting to permit him passage. He evaded Joe's grasping paws again and again, jabbing when he could to hold Guthrie at bay. An opening presented itself. Uncoiling like a bullwhip, he delivered an uppercut that sent the man tottering.

The onlookers had fallen silent, And in that deathly stillness, mocking laughter from the doorway of the saloon seemed doubly loud. "Oh, the joy! I would have paid money to see this! The great Rowdy Joe has met his match at last!" Luke Olinger shook his cane in glee. For someone who claimed to be Guthrie's business associate, he took uncommon delight in seeing his partner humbled.

Rowdy Joe paused. "Keep it up and you're next! I don't care what he says. There's only so much I'll take, bastard."

"Were I you," Luke said, then lowered his voice as if talking to himself to say, "and thank God I'm not,"—he raised his voice again—"I wouldn't worry about someone having a few chuckles at your expense. I'd worry about the fact that by tonight everyone in Dew Claw and all the prospectors on all the creeks for miles around will have heard that you're not as tough as they've always feared. Your reputation will be tarnished, you lumbering ox. And without it, what use are you to anyone? If you get my meaning."

Furrows lined Rowdy Joe's forehead. He was thinking, and the strain showed. "We can't have that, can we?" Straightening, he folded his arms across his chest.

Fargo had listened to the exchange, as puzzled as everyone else by a few of the comments. Seeing Guthrie relax, he jumped to the conclusion the fight was over and started to lower his fists. It was a costly mistake.

"Mundy!" the bull thundered.

Nina's shout a split-second later was a split second too late. Fargo heard a swish, felt something swoop down around his shoulders. He tried to twist and leap out from under it, but the loop constricted like a band of steel and he was jerked off his feet with breathtaking speed. His shoulder crashed onto the ground, his hat went flying. Mud splattered his face and neck as he was pulled down the street at the end of a rope. One of the four horsemen at the hitch rail had lassoed him as neatly as could be.

The other three trotted alongside, laughing and joking. Fargo felt little pain, but only because the mud was soft enough to swim in. He fumbled at his Colt, unable to grip it. The rider who had roped him looked over a shoulder, then wheeled his zebra dun and galloped toward the crowd. Fargo tensed, but the sudden snap jarred him to the bone anyway. He flew back the way they had come, mud spurting into his mouth, into his nose, into his eyes. He could barely see. Pounding hooves hammered his eardrums. He figured they would drag him clear out of the camp, but to his surprise he slid to a lurching halt somewhere near the saloon.

Fargo began to rise to his knees. Agony spiked him as a heavy boot slammed onto his spine, smashing him flat. A hand pressed against the back of his head and mashed his face into the muck. He had no time to suck in air. His breath was choked off. He surged upward but he could not get enough leverage. Helpless, he was completely at Rowdy Joe's mercy. The boot shifted and a low growl sounded in his ear.

"Listen good, jackass. I should kill you right here and now. Snap your back like a dry twig. But we're not supposed to kill anyone unless we get permission first. So I'm going to make an example of you, instead."

Fargo's lungs were close to bursting. He had to breathe or he would die. Bunching his legs, he was set to propel himself upward at all costs when Rowdy Joe's huge hands seized him by the shoulders and flipped him over. Mud covered both eyes. He could not see. Blinking furiously, he glimpsed daylight. Then a ten-ton boulder came crashing down on his chest.

"That's for taking my hitch rail."

Another kick about busted Fargo's lower ribs. Instinctively, he sought to double over, but hands on his arms prevented him.

"That was for knocking one of my teeth loose."

Waves of pain flooded Fargo. He could not think, could not even focus. A tiny inner voice screamed at him to move, to get out of there before Guthrie kicked him again. But his limbs were mush.

"And this one is for the hell of it."

A boot rammed into Fargo's stomach. Bitter bile rose in his throat as he thrashed and sputtered. Other feet kicked him, battering his head and torso and legs, kicking again and again and again, until the torture crested in an avalanche of unspeakable anguish. Then a strange thing happened. His mind seemed to detach itself from his body. He lost all sensation and felt as if he were adrift on a cloud. The blows kept landing but he no longer was racked by torment.

How long it went on, Fargo could not say. Cruel laughter signaled the end of the beating. Footsteps clomped off. People spoke, but in soft tones. He wanted to sit up and couldn't. Involuntarily, he flinched when fingers closed on his wrists.

"It's me. Nina. Don't worry. I'll get you out of here." To someone else she said, "Stay put while I fetch the wagon."

"What if they come back out to hurt him some more?" That was Mandy, fear in every syllable.

"They won't. They'll be too busy celebrating. Now do as I say."

A small hand slipped into Fargo's own and gently squeezed. "Hang on, mister. You leave everything to us." Mandy paused. "You *are* alive, aren't you?"

Truth to tell, Fargo half wished he wasn't. He hurt from head to toe. Every square inch. Every joint. Every muscle. Every nerve. He still could not see anything. His lips were as heavy as lead but he forced them to move. "I think so."

Mandy tittered nervously. "Goodness gracious. You had me real worried. They stomped on you something awful."

Fargo wanted to tell her they would pay. That if it was the last thing he ever did, he would give Rowdy Joe Guthrie and Guthrie's men a taste of their own medicine. But he was too weak, in too much agony. He lay still, drifting in and out of awareness until the noisy clatter of wagon wheels roused him. Someone slipped arms under his and hoisted him up off the ground, grunting.

"Damn," Nina declared. "You're all muscle. Help me out. I can't lift you alone."

It took every shred of willpower Fargo had, but he locked his knees so his legs were rigid and sturdy, and shuffled where she guided him. When she said to lie back, he did. His groping fingertips made contact with the bed of a wagon. There was a jumble of movement, of noises he did not bother to sort out. A horse nickered. Something nuzzled his right leg. Mandy's small hand slipped into his again as the wagon jolted forward.

"We're on our way," the girl said. "Another hour and we'll have you safe."

"Thank you." Fargo could feel the mud that caked his eyes hardening. Blinking would not loosen it so he weakly raised his hand to pry it off.

"What are you trying to do?" Mandy demanded. "Oh."
She pushed his arm aside and carefully peeled the blinding
gunk away, a delicate task with the wagon bouncing and
swaying as it was. Bit by gradual bit the rose glow of late afternoon blossomed overhead. Her sweetly innocent face
hovered above his like that of a cherub. "There. All done.
How's that?"

"Fine."

She leaned on his chest, growing sad. "I'm so sorry. I was
fit to cry. But I warned you, didn't I? I told you that was Mr.
Guthrie's hitch rail, that no one but him is ever allowed to
use it. Didn't I?"

"Yes. You did."

"Why wouldn't you listen?" Mandy picked more mud off.
"You must be a lot like me. My pa always said that whatever
he told me went in one of my ears and out the other. And he
warned me that one day it would get me into a heap of trouble." She leaned closer. "Did your pa say the same to you
when you were little?"

"I don't rightly remember."

"Why not? You're not that old." She wiped a brown glob
from the crest of his nose. "You don't have kids of your own
yet, do you?"

Fargo did not see what that had to do with anything.
"No."

"Didn't think so. You don't have any gray hairs. And Pa
always claimed you can tell who has kids by their gray
hairs."

Mandy chirped on, relating how her family had trekked
westward across the vast plains. How she had been so scared
of the immense buffalo herds and the Indians. How once a
bolt of lightning set the prairie on fire and they were lucky
to escape with their lives.

Fargo stopped listening. He did not mean to ignore her
but fatigue gnawed at him like a beaver on soft bark. He had
been up since before dawn. The previous night, he'd slept

only four hours. More than anything, he craved rest. Deep, undisturbed slumber.

The next moment, sleep claimed him.

The touch of a palm on Skye Fargo's forehead snapped him out of an inky emptiness into the bright light of day. In pure reflex his own hand shot up and seized the wrist of the person who had touched him. There was a sharp intake of breath. He stared up into narrowed eyes as lake-blue as his own. Rich raven tresses framed features that resembled Nina's, only this woman's lips were fuller, her eyebrows arched higher, her nose was thinner. She had the same ripe figure, clothed in a form-fitting beige shirt and faded pants that clung to her fine legs.

"Is this any way to treat someone who has watched over you for the past twenty-four hours?" she asked in a voice that dripped honey.

"Twenty-four?" Fargo repeated, shocked. Letting go, he rose onto his elbows. He was lying on a cot, in a tent, and swaddled in blankets. He did not need to lift them to know he was naked.

"You were out to the world," the woman said. "We cleaned you up, and Nina washed your clothes. They're out on the line. They should be dry if you want me to fetch them."

"And you are?"

She brushed at her hair. A simple movement, yet so graceful. So alluring. "Oh, Sorry. I reckon I should introduce myself. Ella Youngblood, at your service. Nina and Mandy are my sisters, in case you didn't know."

No one had mentioned their last name. Fargo had to admit it was fitting. "Did you undress me yourself?"

Ella blushed as readily as her siblings. A family trait, evidently. "Nina helped. Don't worry. We didn't indulge ourselves." Her grin was impish. "Not that we weren't tempted. It isn't often we have a man completely at our mercy. If

Mandy hadn't been right outside, you might have gotten lucky and never even known it."

Fargo liked brazen women. They were usually much more fun to be with, and much more lively under the sheets. Then again, sometimes it was the shy ones who were bubbling volcanoes inside, just waiting for the right man to come along and shatter the dam that held their blazing passions in check. There was no predicting. Casting for a woman was a lot like casting for a fish. A man threw in his line and hoped for the best. Sometimes he hooked a tasty trout. Sometimes the hook came up empty.

"I'll get your buckskins," Ella offered, rising. She got no further.

The tent flap parted and in walked Nina, the clothes in question draped over a forearm. "I heard you talking," she explained as she placed them on the cot.

With the pair side by side, the family resemblance was even more striking. So were the differences. Nina was taller, Ella's bust a shade fuller. Both were bronzed from long hours spent working outdoors. Both had a sensual charm that oozed from every pore. Both were genuine beauties. And both made Fargo's mouth water.

"Where's Mandy?" Ella asked.

Nina motioned. "Playing by the sluice trough. Don't get yourself in a dither. Felix is guarding her. She'll be fine."

Ella turned. "I don't like leaving her alone. Not with those vultures out to get us. Not after what they did to Pa." Smiling at Fargo, she said, "Supper is in an hour. The washbasin is right outside and to the left. Spare towels are under the cot you're on. You can help yourself." She crooked a finger at her sister. "Let's leave him be. He'll want his privacy."

"Oh, I doubt that," Nina said with a playful wink. "Skye wouldn't mind at all if one of us stayed and helped him dress. Would you, handsome?"

Fargo was not given the opportunity to answer. Ella gripped her sister's elbow and pushed Nina from the tent, remarking as they went, "You'll have to forgive her. She's the hussy in our family."

Fargo had a lot to ponder. He'd had no desire to get involved in the storm brewing in Dew Claw, but the beating had changed his outlook. It was personal now. He had a grudge to settle. Beyond that, he had a keen interest in helping the Youngbloods. They had put their own lives at risk by aiding him when no one else would. It had taken great courage on Nina's and Mandy's part to trundle him out of the mining camp.

He dressed slowly. He had to. His arms were unbearably sore, his chest covered with bruises. His shoulders black and blue. All the mud was gone. So someone had washed him while he slept. Ella? Nina? Or both? Tugging on his boots proved hardest. One of his ankles was swollen but he could walk without a limp.

His hat and gunbelt were nowhere to be seen. On a hunch he peered under each of the other two cots and found them under the last, on a folded blanket. Throwing a towel over a shoulder, he stepped outside, squinting against the glare.

The sun was about where it had been when he passed out in the wagon, which was parked nearby. A stone's throw away was a gurgling creek. Beside a sluice crouched Mandy, digging in the dirt. Observing her antics was an old hound with floppy ears and a sloped back. The horses were tethered where they could graze, along a grassy strip that grew at the base of a low cliff flanking the tent.

From up and down the creek rose a babble of voices, punctuated by the ring of metal on stone. For as far as the eye could see in both directions were prospectors busy at their claims, either panning or tending sluices or digging. They were packed so close together that Fargo could not see how they knew whose claim was whose. Stakes helped. So did ropes strung from tall poles.

Ella was filing the washbasin. "That's Dead Cow Creek yonder," she informed him, lowering the bucket. "Named after a cow that belonged to the man who made the first strike hereabouts. Seems it had wandered off so he went searching and found it dead, killed by a cougar. He was carving up what was left of the meat when he spotted some color in a pool. The rest, as they say, is history."

"Where is he now?" Fargo idly inquired.

"Dead. Just like our pa."

Fargo rolled his left sleeve up to his elbow, then his right. The water was cold but refreshing. He splashed it on his face, on his neck, then dried off. When he turned, all three Youngblood sisters were studying him as if they had never seen a man before. "What's wrong, ladies?"

Mandy was close to tears again. "You wash up just like our pa always did." Her lower lip trembled as it was wont to do, a sure sign she was under stress. "You're a lot like he was. Except you have a beard, he didn't. And he wouldn't ever wear buckskins. They made his skin itch."

Fargo had worn nothing *but* buckskins most of his life. As for how he washed, he imagined a lot of people did it the same way. The sisters missed their father so much, they were seeing traits of his where none really existed. But Fargo could not bring himself to tell them that. "I'm flattered, little one. I take it your father was a good man."

"The best." This from Nina. "He seldom drank, hardly ever cussed. And he never mistreated us girls. Even after we lost Ma."

"He'd do anything for us," Ella added. "Make any sacrifice. He was the biggest, kindest, gentlest soul you'd ever meet."

"Pa loved us and we loved him," Mandy said simply, summing up the depth of their affection.

Fargo recalled what she had revealed in Dew Claw. "He died two weeks ago?"

"It's been twelve days," Nina said sorrowfully. "He went to town to pay off the debt we owed Mr. Cavendar and never came back. The next day we hunted high and low, and once word got out, practically all the gold seekers along Dead

Cow Creek helped out. It was one of them who found part of Pa's shirt, covered with dry blood."

"What killed him?"

Mandy sniffled. "I told you, remember? Some say it was a bear. Some say it was a big cat."

"What did the tracks say?"

The sisters exchanged glances.

"Tracks?" Ella said.

"There had to be prints," Fargo said. A grizzly was one of the heaviest creatures on the North American continent. It left footprints in the hardest of soil. Mountain lions were much lighter and tread softly, but even they left telltale spoor a competent tracker could read. "What kind were at the spot where the shirt was found?"

The older Youngbloods fidgeted as if embarrassed. "There weren't any animal tracks," Nina said. "Some of the older men looked and looked, and couldn't understand it. Others said the ground was too rocky."

"I'd like one of you to take me there tomorrow morning," Fargo said. He had spied his saddle on a flat boulder. The Henry was still in the scabbard. He ambled over, three shadows flitting at his heels.

"Does this mean you're fixing to help us?" Mandy asked.

"It does."

Before Fargo could so much as blink, he was being warmly hugged by all three. Mandy had him around the knees, Nina's arms were looped about his waist, and Ella was at his side, hers wrapped around his chest. His bruises flared in protest but he did not object. Rather, he savored the warmth of the older two, savored the pressure of their breasts and the feel of Ella's hips against his. It was enough to make a man giddy.

"Thank you! Thank you! Thank you!" the child exclaimed. "No one else will lift a finger to help us anymore."

Ella explained. "It's not that they don't like us. They have their claims to work. Every day they miss costs them money."

Nina was more critical. "That's only part of the reason. They're afraid that if they pry into Pa's death, the same thing will happen to them. Our father wasn't the first. Seven men have died so far. And not a trace of any of them, except for the scrap of material we have."

Fargo noticed that Mandy had stepped back but her sisters lingered. Ella's hands had slipped low enough to almost brush a part of him that any self-respecting prim and proper lady would rather die than touch, while Nina's fingernails were tracing light circles on his lower back. Between the two of them, they set his groin to twitching. He had to peel himself loose before he made a spectacle of himself. "Can I see the scrap?"

Mandy darted into the tent.

"I don't want you to get your hopes up," Fargo said quickly while she was gone. "I'll do what I can. But I can't make any promises. Whatever is going on, those behind it are careful not to make mistakes."

"Anything you can do will be appreciated," Nina said, reaching out to stroke the back of his hand. An innocent enough act, yet ripe with hidden promise. To accent her point, she added, "I don't know how I'll ever be able to thank you enough."

Ella rolled her eyes.

In the shake of a lamb's tail little Mandy returned. In her palms she bore the piece of fabric, holding it as if it were the most precious jewel in all the world. Fargo could guess why. It was special, one of the very last things her father came in contact with. "Here it is."

The scrap had no buttons or stitches to give Fargo a clue as to which part of the garment it came from. Originally, it had been a blue and gray plaid, typical of work shirts the prospectors favored. Blood had stained most of it a dark scarlet. No claw marks were apparent. No bite marks, either. "What was your father's name?"

"Didn't we say?" Ella responded. "Brian."

Fargo had a dozen other questions but they had to wait.

The hound picked that moment to utter a rumbling growl worthy of a rabid wolf. Trotting up Dead Cow Creek were three riders, their broad-brimmed hats and vests and gunbelts setting them apart from those they passed. Some had to scramble out of their path or be trod under. Spiteful gazes were fixed on them by everyone. They were hated, despised, by one and all—and they did not care.

"Oh, God!" Nina breathed.

"Who are they?" Mandy asked.

"Some of the hardcases who ride with Rowdy Joe Guthrie," Ella said. "I recognize the coyote in the lead. His name is Mundy."

Fargo recognized the man, too. It was the son of a bitch who had roped him, the one who had dragged him from one end of the street to the other. Angling to the left so the sisters would not be hit by a stray slug, he planted himself and waited. He had planned to hold off a day or two before he confronted any of those who had humiliated him, so he could rest up. But now was as good a time as any. "Whatever happens next, none of you move."

Mandy's lower lip was quivering once more. "Why, Mr. Fargo? What do you think is going to happen?"

"Someone is going to die."

3

A frontiersman had to learn many skills to survive in the wilderness. Being able to track was just one. Proficiency with a gun and a knife went almost without saying. Equally critical was full knowledge of the many wild things that roamed mountains and plain. Not just what kinds there were, but every little thing about them. What each ate, when they liked to eat it. Where to find their burrows or the places they bedded down. The times of day or night when they were most active. Their mating habits. Every tidbit of information helped a frontiersman to survive that much better.

Knowing the habits of his fellow men was another needed talent. Not just what they did but *why* they did what they did; what *kind* of men they were. Being able to tell a decent man from a cutthroat. The savvy to recognize when someone was a threat and when someone was not. To have the knack, as it were, to peer into the depths of a man's soul, to read others like the proverbial book.

Skye Fargo had honed his ability to read others to a razor's edge. Little things, such as how a man dressed, how he moved, what type of weapons he favored and how he wore his gunbelt or carried a rifle, revealed volumes. Such as now.

The three men who approached bore the hardened stamp of seasoned killers. All three had eyes as flinty as quartz. They rode coiled in the saddle, like sidewinders about to strike. Haughty stares, laced with arrogance and scorn, were directed at the prospectors.

Which was fitting for men who saw themselves as better than everyone else. Or, rather, *deadlier*. These were killers, men who lived by their weapons and their wits. Men who would slay at the drop of a hat, for no real reason other than to satisfy their lust to spill blood. They were rabid wolves in human guise.

The trio came to within thirty feet of the tent, then drew rein. The tallest, Mundy, wore a Remington on his left hip, the butt slanted forward for a cross draw. On his saddle was a coiled rope, the same rope he had used to drag Fargo. Leering, he roved his gaze over Ella and Nina, undressing them. "Nice to see you again, ladies," he said in a voice reminiscent of gravel grating on tin.

"Too bad we can't say the same," Ella retorted. "What are you and those other two coyotes doing here? I don't recollect inviting any vermin to supper."

Mundy's mouth curled in an oily smile. "Feisty filly, ain't you? I like that in a gal. I like it when they scratch and kick and scream." He winked at Nina, then focused on Fargo. "But we're not here to pay a social call. We came to see your friend. Rowdy Joe heard a rumor that you'd carted him out of town, and he wanted to know if it was true." Mundy leaned on his saddle horn. "To be honest, mister, I figured you'd be food for the worms along about now. Not many hombres could take the beatin' you did and live to tell about it."

Fargo did not respond. He was gauging how dangerous the other two were. The man on the right was heavyset and slovenly dressed. Droopy jowls and slack shoulders gave him the look of one of those overfed city-bred dogs who were too lazy to lift a paw to scratch themselves. Fargo did not rate him as much of a threat, despite the Smith & Wesson strapped to his right hip.

The third rider was cut from different cloth. Meanness clung to him like a shroud. A bean pole, he had the whipcord tough bearing of someone who did not care one whit for anyone other than himself. He had used the two pistols at his waist before and would gladly do so again. His hands hung loose at his sides, his elbows slightly bent. He grinned, but his grin was as coldly evil as his eyes. This was the one to watch, Fargo decided.

Mundy shifted his weight, his saddle creaking. "What's the matter, mister? Cat got your tongue? I'm talkin' to you and you don't have the courtesy to answer? I don't think I like you much."

Fargo resented being toyed with as if he were a rank greenhorn. "Who gives a damn what you like?"

The tall gunman chuckled and glanced at the beanpole. "Did you hear that, Rickert? We've got us a regular hellion by the tail."

Rickert did not answer, or move. He was poised for one thing and one thing alone, and he did not let anything distract him.

The heavyset man, though, had a comment to make. Guffawing, he said, "He don't look like no hellion to me, Mundy. We stomped him once, we can lick him again. Or blow out his lamp, if it comes to that, like Joe told us to do."

Mundy was displeased. "Do you ever use your head for anything besides a hat rack, Bob?" he sniped.

"What did I do?" Bob said, confused. He was too dull-witted to realize he had just made a statement in front of witnesses that would put the blame squarely on Guthrie's shoulders if they were to gun Fargo down.

"Just keep your mouth shut," Mundy ordered. "The only thing it's good for, anyway, is guzzlin' coffin varnish." He straightened but kept his right hand on the saddle horn, close to the Remington's pearl grips. "Now, stranger. How soon can you leave?"

"I'm going somewhere?" Fargo rejoined.

"That you are. Rowdy Joe thinks you're a troublemaker. And he doesn't like troublemakers. So he'd like for you to mount up and light a shuck for wherever you want. Just so you're gone by, say, tomorrow morning. It'll give you another night to rest up. That's fair, ain't it?"

"You're all heart."

"Don't get snippy. Just do as you're told and no one has to get hurt. We'll be back in the morning to hurry you along in case you are a lot more stupid than you seem." Confident he would be obeyed, Mundy lifted his reins.

"There's no need to come back," Fargo said. He had made up his mind to settle it now rather than risk having them take him off guard the next day.

"Oh? And why is that?"

"Because I'm not going anywhere. Ride back and tell your boss that he should have left well enough alone. He should have let me leave Dew Claw in peace. Now I intend to stick around awhile."

Mundy sighed. "You're makin' a big mistake, stranger. Rowdy Joe is one of the three most important men in these parts. When he tells someone to jump through a hoop, they jump. No sass. No questions asked." His smile became oilier. If that were possible. "Do us both a favor and change your mind. I'd hate to have to ride all the way out here again just so we can use you for target practice."

"Oh, I wouldn't worry about that."

"No?"

"None of you will shoot anyone."

"Why not? Are we going to get religion all of a sudden?"

Fargo shook his head. "You won't have any guns to shoot with. I want all three of you to unhitch your gunbelts and drop them. Then slide your rifles out and let them fall, too. Nice and slow. I'll leave them with Cavendar at the mercantile when I leave in a day or two. You can pick them up there."

Mundy snickered. "Anyone ever tell you what a great sense of humor you have, mister? You expect us to turn our irons over to you, just like that?"

"Yes."

Mundy's features grew as hard as Rickert's. "Either you're plumb loco, or you've got more sand in you than an hourglass. Either way, you know we're not going to do it.

Not if we want to go on holdin' our heads high like real men should."

Yes, Fargo had known as much. He had foreseen what would occur the moment he laid eyes on the three hardcases. Which was why he had told Mandy someone was going to die. Those who lived by the gun would rather die by the gun than part with theirs. "Is Guthrie worth dying for? Does he pay you that much?"

"I could make more money ridin' sign for a one-horse outfit," Mundy said. "But honest work always has bored me silly. And how much we pocket ain't neither here nor there. All that counts is at the moment we ride for Joe Guthrie, and he gave us orders we're obliged to carry out."

"Then I guess there's nothing left to say."

"No, there ain't."

It was Rickert, not Mundy, who went for his six-gun first. Mundy was a fraction slower. Both were fast, though, very fast. Both had practiced and practiced to where they could unlimber a pistol as slick as greased lightning. Their hands were blurs as their revolvers flashed up and out. And it was hard to say which one of them was the more surprised to learn they were not quite fast enough. For even as they cleared leather, they were staring down the barrel of a cocked Colt.

Rickert was the quicker of the pair so he was the one Fargo shot first. The bean pole rocked backward, the slug taking him high in the chest. Mortally wounded but still able to dispense death, Rickert attempted to level his Smith & Wesson. A second shot cored his skull from front to back, flipping him into the dust.

Fargo pivoted, firing again at the same instant Mundy did. The tall gunman missed. Fargo didn't. Scorching lead smashed into the tall gunman's ribs and exploded from his back in a gory spray. Mundy swayed, upright but dead, the light of life fading rapidly. His horse bolted.

That left heavyset Bob, who grabbed at his pistol with a speed that could only be compared to frozen molasses.

Fargo took two steps, extending the Colt and aiming it at the man's head. "Don't!"

Bob imitated stone, his pistol half drawn, his skin pasty pale. Beads of sweat broke out on his brow. "I . . . I . . . I . . ." he blurted in undisguised terror.

"Shuck the gunbelt and the rifle," Fargo directed. His trigger finger was curved around the trigger; the slightest pressure and the Colt would go off. He did not ease the tension until the cutthroat had done as he demanded, and then, sidling closer, he pressed the muzzle against the man's side.

"Please!" Bob whined. "Please, no! I'm begging you!"

"Do you want to live?"

"God Almighty, yes!"

"Then here's what you'll do." Fargo paused. "Go back to Dew Claw. Tell Rowdy Joe what you saw. Tell him that if he sends anyone else after me, they'll get the same. Then you pack your plunder in your war bag and make yourself scarce in these parts. Think you can do all that?"

Bob's chin bobbed vigorously, the fleshy folds rippling like so much pudding. "Sure can. Tell Guthrie. Pack. Get the hell out. No problem. Guthrie can eat my dust, for all I care." He glanced at the ground. "Umm, what about my six-shooter and Spencer? They didn't come cheap."

"Buy new ones at the first town you blow into."

Some people just did not know when they were well off. Bob was one of them. "But you said you'd leave our hardware at the mercantile."

"That was before your pards and you tried to put windows in my skull. Be thankful you're still breathing. Now get the hell out of here. Or maybe I'll see if I can still shoot the ears off a man without killing him."

The incentive spurred the heavyset gunman into wheeling his bay and lighting out as if his britches were aflame. To Fargo's surprise, many of the prospectors along the creek applauded, hooting and hollering to raise the dead. Some even threw stones at Bob's back.

Fargo reloaded the Colt, always the first order of business

after a gunfight. When he was done, he twirled it into his holster, then turned. The Youngblood sisters were staring at him with mixed emotions. Mandy, in awe. Nina, in amazement. Ella, in admiration, tinged with a hint of newborn hunger that had nothing to do with food.

The little one clapped. "You were wonderful, Mr. Fargo! Those bad men had it coming. They were always mean to everybody."

"Where did you learn to use a gun like that?" Nina asked. "I've never seen anyone who can draw and shoot so fast."

Ella's smile veiled a deeper warmth. "I knew there was something special about you. I just knew it. At long last we've found someone who isn't afraid of Guthrie's outfit. Maybe now we can find out what happened to our pa."

Fargo walked to where Rickert lay. Their joy was premature. Rowdy Joe was not about to leave Dew Claw or mend his ways over the loss of two hired guns. Finding replacements was easy. Leather-slappers eager to earn reputations were as common as fleas on a mangy hound dog. Speaking of which, the Youngbloods' mongrel, Felix, was sniffing at the pool of blood that slowly spread outward from Rickert's body. Fargo hiked a boot to kick it but the dog bared its yellowed teeth and growled.

"I wouldn't, were I you," Ella said. "He's liable to take a bite out of your leg."

"He's fought bears before," Mandy boasted. "Once, he tore into a grizzly that was after our team and drove it off. All by his lonesome."

Personally, Fargo doubted the dog could drive off a baby raccoon. But he did not want to upset them, so he said, "Keep him away while we take care of the body."

Nina grabbed Felix by the scruff of his neck and pulled him toward the creek. Which left Ella to assist Fargo in stripping the body of weapons and valuables. They included a thin, square silver case. Ella fiddled with a tiny latch, and the case popped open. She stared, then read softly, "To my dear brother, Clarence, from his devoted sister, Eunice." She swiveled the case. It contained a miniature of a pretty young woman in a homespun dress. The inscription had been engraved on the inside of the lid.

Mandy was horrified. "Oh, mercy! The poor man had a sister?"

As if that somehow made him less of a cold-blooded killer. Fargo bent and grasped Rickert's ankles. He dragged the lifeless husk toward the rear of the camp. Ella stooped to help, taking one of the legs. Their shoulders brushed, their hips pressed close, but she did not seem to mind.

"Look!" Nina suddenly called out.

Fargo spun. Mundy's horse was coming down the creek. Incredibly, the tall gunman was still on the hurricane deck, doubled over at the waist and swaying wildly. A prospector tried to snag the reins but the chestnut skipped aside.

Fargo moved to intercept the animal. It veered to the right, and he took two bounds to cut it off. The chestnut promptly angled toward the creek and would have rushed on around if not for the old hound. Felix abruptly pulled loose from Nina, darted in front of it, and commenced barking. Agitated, the chestnut reversed direction again—running right into Fargo's arms. Clutching the bridle, he held on while the horse whinnied and pranced.

"Did you see what Felix did?" Mandy declared. "Wasn't that smart of him?"

"Pa trained him to help gather up our stock when we were out on the prairie," Nina detailed.

Ella, unbidden, gripped the reins, freeing Fargo to ease Mundy to the ground. Once the body was out of the saddle, the chestnut quieted down. Fargo toted Mundy to the base of the cliff, where the soil did not appear to be as rocky as elsewhere. Probing with his fingers established it was soft enough for their purposes. "I'll need a shovel," he said.

The burial took the better part of an hour. Ella and Nina helped, relieving him after he had dug the first grave. Mandy had charge of the dog, which either had a burning curiosity about the dead or was not being fed enough. Felix would not stop trying to get at the bodies until they were under the ground. He misbehaved so badly, the sisters tied him up.

Twilight cloaked Dead Cow Creek by the time they were done. Fargo piled the weapons and other possessions in the tent and went to the creek to wash up. The older sisters joined him. Dirt caked their fingers and was smeared on their clothes. They were tired and caked with perspiration, yet their beauty shone through their fatigue like shafts of sunlight through clouds. They were as lovely as any St. Louis or New Orleans belle he had ever seen. As ravishing, in their way, as the finest ladies New York or Boston had to offer.

"Will you go into Dew Claw tomorrow?" Nina asked.

"I'd like to see where your father was killed," Fargo reminded her. He would give Rowdy Joe a day or two to stew, then he'd pay Guthrie a visit. It would give his body extra time to mend.

"I'll start supper," Ella announced. Then she gestured angrily. "I plumb forgot. What with all the excitement yesterday, we never did get the new vittles we need. We've hardly any food left."

"Leave that to me," Fargo volunteered. "You just heat some water in a pot."

Mandy had overheard. "I'd give anything for some elk or venison. Or maybe some bear or possum. Or coon or beaver or—"

"She'll eat anything," Nina joked.

"Except snakes," Mandy corrected her. "Pa once killed a rattler for us. But I kept thinking of how it wriggled after he chopped the head off, and I couldn't take a bite."

Fargo had always been fond of snake meat himself. It was similar to chicken, only tastier. "No rattlers tonight. I promise."

Presently, the Henry in hand, Fargo forded the creek. Campfires dotted both banks. Work had largely ceased for the day and the gold seekers were sitting down to enjoy the few quiet hours allotted them. Around a fire downstream an unusual number had congregated. Thirty or more, holding a meeting. He idly wondered what they were up to as he hiked on into the forest.

Almost immediately, Fargo saw that signs of wildlife were missing. The prospectors had killed off all the game close to Dead Cow Creek, their trails crisscrossing one another in a bewildering maze of random wanderings.

If he wanted to eat, he must hunt elsewhere. Accordingly, he steered his sore body toward the adjacent hills, climbing steadily for forty-five minutes. The light was rapidly fading but enough remained to confirm he had acted wisely. Tracks and spoor grew more plentiful the higher he went.

At intervals, shots rang out. Others had the same idea he did, and they'd roamed far afield to fill their bellies. He saw a man on the next slope bring down a fawn. A helpless, tiny fawn. Fargo would rather shoot his own foot off. He liked to flatter himself that no matter how starved he was, he would never stoop so low. But he was only fooling himself. When a person was famished, they would eat *anything*. On several occasions he had proven it by making a meal of grubs, or even less savory morsels. Since Mandy and her sisters were not likely to be partial to creepy, slithery things, he sought something more substantial.

Providence came to his rescue in the form of a spike buck. A black-tail, it was much younger and smaller than those he preferred to shoot, but he could not afford to be choosy. It was too dark. When the deer leaped from out of a thicket less than ten yards away, he brought it down with a single shot. Small though it was, it proved to be quite heavy. To spare his bruised body unnecessary pain, he rigged up a crude travois, lashing limbs together with whangs from his buckskins. No self-respecting Indian would ever use a litter so shabbily constructed, but it sufficed to drag the buck back to camp.

The Youngbloods had a fire going. Mandy had hunkered next to Felix, a thin arm draped over the hound's shoulders.

Nina was cleaning the rifle taken from Rickert, while Ella chopped a type of wild root used for seasoning by settlers and Indians alike. They jumped up when he splashed across. The oldest two wore pistols that had belonged to the gunmen.

"Fixing to fight a war?" Fargo remarked.

"If we have to," Ella said. She patted the Remington. "Next time some polecats show up uninvited, we'll bed them down, permanent-like."

"That we will," Nina agreed. "We're tired of having gun sharks run roughshod over us and everyone else. Tarnation! There are a heap more of us than there are of them. If all the prospectors banded together, Guthrie and Olinger and their crowd wouldn't be able to push us around anymore."

Mandy was thinking only of her empty belly. "How soon can we butcher that buck? I'm so hungry, I could eat it hair and all."

Fargo did the honors. It had been so long since the sisters had eaten a decent meal that they hovered over him like a flock of buzzards. Each one practically drooled as he carved the meat into juicy chunks and dropped them in the boiling water. Soon the delicious aroma of stew filled the air. Mandy squatted next to the fire and impatiently rocked on her heels, her eyes wide, her tiny jaw slack, almost as if she were intoxicated by the smell.

Fargo stirred every so often. Sometimes chunks would bob to the surface, and when that happened the sisters leaned toward the pot as if they yearned to dive in. When he ladled out a small piece to test whether it was done, Nina and Ella both licked their rosy lips in anticipation. The meat was pink in the center, but Fargo figured it had cooked long enough. "Help yourselves, ladies."

All three were ready, bowls and big wooden spoons in their hands. Mandy attacked the stew as if it were trying to eat her instead of the other way around. In her haste she spilled some hot broth on her arm but she did not cry out.

She gulped greedily, mewing like a kitten, barely taking the time to chew.

Ella and Nina were little better. Each filled her bowl to the brim and then *drank* from it. They chewed with relish, closing their eyes and moaning as if they were swept up in sexual ecstasy rather than partaking of a simple supper.

Fargo let them savor two helpings before he helped himself. There was plenty of meat left should they empty the pot.

The chirp of crickets and the yip of distant coyotes was a constant reminder of the vast wilderness that surrounded them. Overhead, a myriad of sparkling stars sprinkled the firmament. From the northwest wafted a stiff breeze. To the east a quarter-moon hove into sight, bathing the majestic mountains in a silvery sheen.

Quiet reigned along Dead Cow Creek. Fargo ate his fill and leaned back, for the moment at peace with the world. A rare treat for him. Violence and bloodshed were so frequent a part of his life that he had taken to viewing them as the usual state of affairs. He tended to forget most people went from the womb to the grave without someone or something trying to kill them. He forgot that for most folks a sheltered life of ease was the norm. A life where their greatest worry was what clothes they would wear the next day, or how their hair looked, or whether they had gained too much weight.

"Oh, look at her. Such a sweet angel," Ella commented.

Fargo sat up. Mandy had curled into a ball by the fire and was sound asleep. He offered to carry her into the tent.

"I will," Nina volunteered.

As she sluggishly rose, boots tramped in the night. Many boots, coming closer. Fargo leaped erect and tucked the Henry to his shoulder. His first thought was that Rowdy Joe Guthrie had sent others to take up where Mundy and Rickert had fallen short, but the approaching knot of men lit by torches were not gunmen. They were prospectors. He counted a baker's dozen, none of whom were armed. In their lead was a redwood of a man in a dirty flannel shirt and stained denim overalls.

"Harvey Barclay!" Nina declared. "What's the meaning of this? Are you all drunk, to come calling at this late an hour?"

The prospectors halted. Barclay removed his hat. Ruggedly built, sporting a bushy red beard and a square jaw, he did not appear to be the kind of man who was afraid of anything. Yet he nervously wrung the hat, then coughed. "Don't unleash that cat's tongue of yours on us, Nina Youngblood. We apologize for imposing. But it isn't you we've come to see. It's your friend, here."

Ella rose. "What on earth for? What's so important that it can't wait until morning?"

Barclay was reluctant to answer until one of the other men jabbed him. "We've held a meeting and reached a decision. Runners were sent all up and down the creek to inform everyone. It's unanimous."

Nina placed her hands on her hips. "What are you babbling about? No runner came to our camp."

"What decision?" Ella demanded.

The leader of the prospectors jabbed a thumb at Fargo. "It's involves this gent. We're taking up a collection. We'd like to hire him to kill Rowdy Joe Guthrie."

4

Skye Fargo had done many things in his time. He had scouted for the army. He had guided wagon trains across the prairie. He had ridden point for cattle herds, escorted rich Europeans on a big game hunt, led a naturalist on a search for a rare bird, helped the Corps of Topographical Engineers map unexplored territory. He had done all this, and much more. But one thing he had never done, one thing he swore he would never do, was work as a hired killer. He would never sell his skill with a six-shooter, never gun others down for profit. He refused to stoop that low. He refused to taint his very soul.

So now, as the Youngblood sisters and Harvey Barclay and the rest of the prospectors looked at him expectantly, Fargo lowered the Henry, turned, and sat back down. "You've got the wrong man. Find someone else to earn your blood money."

Barclay and the gold hunters came around in front of him, keeping a respectful distance. "Hear us out. Please. That's all we ask."

Nothing they could say or do would sway Fargo in any way, but he nodded curtly. "It's your breath. If you want to waste it, be my guest."

Barclay hesitated again, as if wrestling inwardly to find the right words. "We realize we have no right to impose. But we've all heard what happened in Dew Claw. And many of us saw those gun sharks brace you today. So it's safe to assume Rowdy Joe Guthrie is not one of your favorite people."

"You could say that, yes," Fargo allowed dryly, while helping himself to the little bit of stew left. All the men wore such hopeful expressions, it bothered him a bit to think he must disappoint them so severely.

Barclay's confidence soared. "Well then, our proposition makes sense, doesn't it? Guthrie has been a thorn in our side for months. And he's your enemy, too. You must want to get even with him after what his bunch did. So why not do it and ride off with some spending money in your saddlebags? We've scraped together every spare nugget and poke of dust we have." He paused, then announced, "We can afford to pay you five thousand dollars."

Fargo whistled. That was a lot of money by any standard. He made a comment to that effect.

Barclay was all smiles, thinking he had the deal sewn up. "Sure is. Think of the swell times you can have. Think of all the stuff you can spend it on. Hell, mister, five thousand is more than most folks earn in ten years of busting their backs. And all you have to do is kill a son of a bitch you want to kill anyway. Do we have an agreement?"

"Not so fast." Fargo stuck a piece of meat in his mouth and thoughtfully chewed. "There must be hundreds of prospectors working the creeks in this area. Why not have one of them take care of Guthrie?"

"We've considered that," Barclay admitted. "But we're not gunmen. None of us would stand a prayer."

"The miners must outnumber Guthrie's crowd ten to one," Fargo estimated. "Just march into Dew Claw and run them off."

Some of Barclay's confidence seeped from his face. He began wringing his hat again. "A lot of us would die. An awful lot. And there's no guarantee we'd kill them all. Guthrie might come back with even more hardcases to back him up."

"So what you're saying"—Fargo did not mince words—

"is that you want me to do something none of you have the stomach for."

"I suppose you could say that, yes," Barclay conceded, "but you have to see it from our point of view. None of us have ever killed anyone. Hell, we hardly ever use a gun except to shoot something to eat."

Fargo had no doubt the man was telling the truth. Proficiency with a pistol or rifle did not come easily. It took days and weeks and months of practice, practice, practice. Time most men spent simply earning a living.

The spokesman had gone on. "Another thing to consider is that the majority of us are family men. Three-fourths of us have wives and kids waiting in Denver or in the States. They're depending on us to make it back alive." He then asked, almost accusingly, "Do you have a family, mister?"

The gall of some people! Fargo thought. He keenly resented being manipulated, being made to feel guilty so he would cave in and agree. "No. But whether I do or not isn't what counts. What matters is standing up to Guthrie. Wife or no wife, kids or no kids, there comes a time when a man has to stand on his own two feet. If he *is* a man."

Harvey Barclay shifted his weight from foot to foot. "That's uncalled-for. None of us are yellow. Maybe if you had a family of your own, you'd understand."

The trouble was, Fargo did understand. Any man who had a wife he loved and children he adored did not want to leave them to fend for themselves in a world that was too often cold and cruel. Especially on the frontier, where having a husband and a father could mean the difference between a halfway decent life and miserable poverty. Women left on their own found it hard to make ends meet. Good jobs were few and far between. Many wound up scrubbing floors for pennies, or else were forced to live as soiled doves. Their spirits crushed, their prospects dim, they took to drink. Misery was their daily lot. Their only release, oblivion.

Fargo looked up. The prospectors were all staring at him. "I don't kill for money," he stated flatly.

"Not even for five thousand?" one of them asked.

"Not even for ten thousand."

A pudgy man whose bald pate shone in the firelight coughed and said, "Excuse me for pryin', stranger." He pointed upstream. "My claim is yonder a short ways. I saw Mundy and those other two try to buck you out in gunsmoke today. You must be fixin' to call Guthrie out over it. So why not earn some money for doing what you'll do anyway?"

"My fight with Rowdy Joe is my own affair," Fargo said. "It has nothing to do with you. Any of you."

Barclay grunted. "So that's it. You don't give a tinker's damn about us. What's it matter if honest men are disappearing? All you care about is yourself."

Fargo slowly rose, thunder crackling on his brow. Some of the prospectors stepped back. Others blanched. To Barclay, he said, "Be real careful who you insult. If I were the bastard you make me out to be, you'd have a few slugs in you right about now."

"I didn't mean—" the redwood said, and fell silent.

Fargo simmered down. He had to remember these men were desperate. And men who were at the end of their rope sometimes said and did things they would never do under normal circumstances. "Nina told me seven prospectors have vanished without a trace so far."

"Yes, sir," Barclay responded. "Good, honorable Argonauts they were. Like her pa, Brian. God rest his poor soul. Men who would never just up and traipse off without saying a word to someone."

"Her father had about thirty dollars on him when he went missing. What about the others?"

"I know what you're thinking. But robbery can't have been the motive. Half of those who disappeared hardly had two cents to their name."

Fargo was puzzled. If someone, namely Guthrie, was going around killing gold hounds, there had to be a reason. There had to be something in it for Rowdy Joe. "What about their claims? Has anyone taken them over?"

"No. It couldn't be done. All claims are duly filed with the recorder in Dew Claw. Anyone trying to steal one would be strung up." Barclay elaborated. "We're not gold-blind simpletons. We're doing this the way it ought to be done. Some of us, like Brian Youngblood, were with the forty-niners."

Fargo glanced at Ella and Nina. They had neglected to mention their father was part of the great horde that swarmed to the California goldfields twelve years ago. Thousands had struck it rich. Stories about some of them were still bandied about in saloons and taverns. Such as the prospector who tethered his mule to a wooden stake for the night. When he yanked up the stake the next day, gold flakes coated it. Or the three Frenchmen who uprooted a pesky tree that sat in the middle of their claim, only to find the hole laced with gold. And then there was the little girl who brought a pretty rock she had found to her parents. It turned out to be a seven-pound nugget.

There were many more tales. But for each person who reaped a small fortune, hundreds wound up busted. For every success there were uncounted tragedies. Men who lost everything, even their lives. Men who were overcome by sickness. Men who were robbed. Men who were cheated. Men who lost their minds to gold fever.

Barclay had more to impart. "Early on, we held a big meeting and picked a committee to run things. The men you see here are the ones who were elected. I'm the president. We set up rules for everyone to follow, to make things fair. The same rules the forty-niners had." He rambled them off. "Only one claim per creek per person. Claims can be no larger than a hundred square feet. On placers it can go from bank to bank, otherwise, no. Every claim must be marked. Every claim must be filed with the recorder. No one can dump waste or rocks on another's claim. No water can be diverted other than through a sluice."

Fargo agreed the rules were fair to one and all. But Barclay wasn't finished.

"Every claim has to be worked at least one day a month

or the owner forfeits it. Claims can be bought and sold, but the sale has to be witnessed by at least two others who have no stake in it. Claim jumping, it goes without saying, is not allowed. Anyone caught will be tried and hung. Neither will theft or murder be tolerated."

Fargo knew how miners' courts operated. The culprit was held at gunpoint while a judge and jury were selected. Sometimes a defender and a prosecutor were picked to present evidence for and against the accused. Jury deliberations seldom lasted more than an hour. Punishment was swift. Those found guilty were immediately made guests of honor at a necktie social. And the jury usually provided the rope. He did not see how anyone could steal any of the claims along Dead Cow Creek or elsewhere without being caught and strung up.

"Guthrie must know all this," Fargo mused aloud. "So it wouldn't make sense for him to be behind the disappearances. What does he think to gain?"

"Who else could it be?" Barclay countered. "The rowdy element is under his thumb. Not one of them dares lift a finger against us without his say-so."

"What about Luke Olinger?" Fargo wondered.

"The owner of the Timberline? Why would he stoop to murdering some of us for a few paltry dollars when he's making money hand over fist? Between the watered-down drinks he sells, the cardsharps who run his gambling tables, and those fancy doves in the back rooms, he makes hundreds a day."

The pudgy man motioned. "We're gettin' off the trail, here. What about it, mister? For the last time, will you kill Rowdy Joe for us?"

"Not for money," Fargo stressed.

"Damn," the man said glumly. "A lot of us were countin' on you."

Sour expressions became contagious. Ella stepped forward and gazed at them in contempt. "How dare you, Art Jessup! And the rest of you! Treating Skye as if he's at fault here! You should be thankful he stood up to Mundy and Rickert. That makes two less maggots we have to deal with."

"We're disappointed, is all," Jessup said.

"Be disappointed in yourselves, not in him," Nina remarked. "He's right. If you weren't so scared, you'd stand up to Guthrie on your own."

Barclay was indignant. "That's easy for you girls to say. No one expects females to go out and get themselves killed. But I should think you'd side with us since your own father is one of those missing."

The two sisters stormed toward him, Ella spearing a finger at his chest. "What does being female have to do with anything? Women have as much gumption as men. More, in most cases, if you ask me."

"That's right!" Nina said. "Haven't we been trying all along to find out what happened to our pa? And who was it helped Fargo when no one else would? We did. Females. Not you high-and-mighty men."

A grizzled specimen in a floppy hat started to push past Harvey. "That's enough! Barney Fiddlemeyer don't take no sass off a woman. Ever. I don't care how old you are. A good switching will teach you to respect your elders."

Ella thrust out her chin in defiance. "I'd like to see you try, you flannel-mouthed old goat. I'll blow your lamp out so quick, it will make your head swim."

Fiddlemeyer stalked forward, heedless of the Remington on her shapely hip. "I've given all seven of my daughters regular switchings their whole lives long, and they've all turned out the better for it."

"Enjoy hitting a girl's bottom, do you?" Nina said. "Why, you aren't nothing but a randy pervert."

An explosion was sure to ensue. Barney Fiddlemeyer was gnashing his teeth in outrage. Some of the other miners were as mad as riled bees. And the sisters had their hands on their shooting irons.

Fargo moved around the fire, between the two sides, and held a hand aloft. "Enough!"

Everyone except Fiddlemeyer froze. He came right over and declared loudly, "Out of my way, mister! You don't booger me. As far as I'm concerned, you're as worthless as a four-card flush—"

He got no further. For as if out of thin air, Fargo's Colt had materialized, the muzzle pressed against the tip of Fiddlemeyer's oversized red nose. "You're leaving. Now. All of you."

Barney Fiddlemeyer did not have the brains God gave a turnip. "Go ahead. Shoot. I dare you. Murder me in front of all my friends. They'll stretch your neck from the nearest cottonwood. I'll have the last laugh when my ghost dances on your grave."

Fargo's bluff had been called. He would never kill an unarmed man. But he could, and did, suddenly hit the prospector across the bridge of the nose hard enough to cause Fiddlemeyer to cry out and stagger back, both gnarled hands clasped to his face. "Next time, I'll break it." Taking a deep breath to calm himself, he said, "We're all tired. Our nerves are raw. Just go. But know this. I aim to find out what happened to Brian Youngblood. And I aim to make whoever is to blame pay."

Delight lit Harvey Barclay's features. "Oh? Wish you'd told us sooner. It would have saved us all this trouble. We're confident Guthrie is behind it. So he's the one who will be held to account."

The men gazed at one another, some smiling slyly. Fargo could guess what they were thinking. He was going to do what they had wanted all along without them having to pay a cent. They were getting the job done for free. Small wonder they departed without protest, chuckling and clapping each other on the back, acting like kids who had raided a cookie jar and not been caught.

"Idiots!" Nina muttered.

Ella was more specific. "Men!"

Fargo was amazed that Mandy had slept through the entire heated exchange. With the utmost care, he tenderly picked the child up and gave her to Nina. "Better tuck her in before she catches her death." As he swiveled, he caught Ella studying him intently. "Something on your mind?"

"You're a strange one."

"How so?"

"I can't figure you out. Most men are easy to read. Like that lecher, Barney. Or Harvey, who is as honest as the day is long but who secretly longs to get in my pants. Or Nina's. It doesn't make any difference to him. He doesn't see us for who we are, just what we are."

The fire needed fuel so Fargo stooped to add limbs. "He came right out and told you that, did he?"

"He didn't have to. No male does. A female always knows. The wolves have a certain hungry glint in their eyes. When they smile, it's more like they're opening their mouth to take a bite out of you. And they always bend over backwards to treat a gal nice, even when she might not deserve it." Ella took a seat across from him. "You're different. You're not a wolf, yet I can tell that if I gave you a smidgen of encouragement, you'd be all over me like a bear on honey."

"And you wouldn't mind one bit."

His bluntness surprised her. She stiffened and her cherry lips parted as if she were about to brand him a bald-faced liar, then her mouth closed and she smirked. "Think you have women all figured out, huh?"

Fargo broke a branch over his knee and placed the two halves in the crackling flames. He did not reply.

"It's a rare male who understands females. Maybe you don't know as much as you believe you do." A chuckle fluttered from her silken throat. "Tell me, oh wise one. What do women want more than anything else in the whole world?"

"The same thing everyone does."

"And what might that be?"

Fargo locked his eyes on hers. "To be happy."

Ella did not say anything for a while. When she did, she seemed to be talking more to herself than to him. "Happiness. A mighty rare condition. As elusive as a butterfly for most of us. We seek it day and night. We get so close sometimes. It's almost in our grasp, and then it does what it always does. It slips through our fingers." She poked a rock with her toe. "Happy is what other people claim to be but no one truly is."

Nina emerged from the tent. For the next hour they made small talk, Fargo learning that their father had gone to the California goldfields alone, leaving them and their mother with an aunt and uncle on a farm in Ohio. Brian Youngblood, apparently, always had a hankering to get rich quick. He'd tried one scheme after another and each ended the same. With him broke, and the family worse off than when he started.

"This last time was the last straw for our ma," Nina mentioned. "When he told us he wanted to grub for gold in the Rockies, she had a fit. She refused. But he begged and begged, and she gave in." The auburn-haired beauty tilted her head skyward. "Her heart wasn't in it, though. Maybe that's why she became so weak and sickly. Maybe that's why she died out there on the plains."

"Don't talk like that," Ella said. "It just happened, is all."

On that sorrowful note the women turned in. Fargo sat by the fire for a long time, pondering. He should get to sleep but he was not really tired. At length, he spread out his blankets over by the cliff. No one was likely to spot him in the inky gloom, but he could see anyone who approached their camp. His saddle for a pillow, he lay on his back and admired the heavenly spectacle. To the west the plaintive howl of a lonesome wolf wavered. Much closer, an owl voiced the eternal question of its kind.

Who, indeed? Fargo reflected. Who was responsible for the rash of disappearances? What was the reason behind them? It had to benefit someone, somewhere, somehow. He'd never heard of murders being committed for the hell of it. Though there was that incident in New York City a year or so ago, where some jasper had gone around strangling women for the sheer thrill. Either the man had been stark-raving mad, or he ate loco weed regularly. Fortunately, lunatics like him were as rare as hen's teeth.

The moon was high in the sky when Fargo rolled onto his side and closed his eyes. Enough thinking for one day. He had to be up at first light. If all went well, he could still make it to Denver within three days.

A rustling noise caused one of the horses to nicker softly. Fargo did not move, even when stealthy footsteps drew near. Keeping his voice low so as not to awaken the others, he said, "You're up late." He had recognized the sound as the tent flap being opened and closed, and he had a good idea who was slinking toward him. But he was wrong. It wasn't the one he expected.

"I couldn't doze off no matter how hard I tried," Nina said quietly. "So I thought I'd come out and see if you were still up. Maybe chat awhile."

Fargo rose onto an elbow. She had traded her homespun clothes for a bulky robe that concealed her charms admirably. But it could not hide the delicate contour of her neck, or the marvelous swell of her bosom. He patted the edge of the top blanket. "Have a seat."

Nina did not hesitate. She sat primly, knees bent, legs tucked under her. Yet she contrived to fiddle with the front of her robe so that it parted slightly. A glimpse of pale skin, swelling outward, tantalized him. She smiled uneasily. "I suppose you're tired of hearing us thank you all the time so I won't do that again."

"I haven't really done anything yet," Fargo said. He caught a whiff of perfume, the kind young ladies could buy in St. Louis, two bottles for a dollar. He also noticed she had brushed her hair so that it flowed over her shoulders like an auburn waterfall.

"Mandy sure has taken a shine to you. She woke up when

Ella and I were turning in, and asked if we could keep you."
Nina's teeth shone as white as pearls.

"I hope she won't be too upset when I go."

Nina was shrewd. Rather than come right out and badger him with questions, she was getting to what she wanted to know in a roundabout fashion. "No chance of you sticking around, then? For Mandy's sake, I mean."

"None at all."

"No matter what happens? What if you decide you like it here? What if you were to grow fond of one of us? Heck, we wouldn't mind putting you up. And with you to help, we could turn our claim into a bonanza."

"I can't stay."

"Can't or won't? Well, it was just a thought." Nina hid her disappointment by fiddling with her robe some more. "Not that it makes a difference to me, you understand. I know how it is. We all have our own lives to live."

"Ever seen tumbleweed?"

Nina's brow knit. "Sure. When we were crossing the prairie. Whenever the wind kicked up, tumbleweeds would go rolling by. Dozens at a time, sometimes, like a herd of buffalo on the move. We used to tie ribbons to some and watch until they tumbled out of sight, wondering who might find them." Nina paused. "Why? Are you saying that you're like a tumbleweed?"

He nodded. "I go wherever the wind blows me."

"There must be someplace you hang your hat when your travels are done."

"I'm not ready to settle down."

Nina shifted, her hips rubbing his. "I don't think I've ever met a man quite like you before, Skye. Most can't wait to be hitched. They want a family. They want a home of their own. A roof over their heads."

Fargo indicated the dazzling firmament. "There's my roof." He patted his saddle. "Here's my home." Raising a hand, he gestured at the Ovaro. "And there's the only family I need."

"A horse?" Nina snickered. "Don't take me wrong, but a stallion is no substitute for a willing woman." She leaned down, her hair falling onto his cheek. "Don't you ever get lonely? Don't you ever yearn for human companionship? What do you do when the nights are long and cold?"

The invitation could not have been more blatant if she had climbed to the top of the cliff and shouted it out for everyone along Dead Cow Creek to hear. Fargo glanced at the tent, insuring the flap was closed. Then he slowly elevated an arm, hooked it over her neck, and pulled her face down to his. "I do this," he said, and molded his hot mouth to hers.

Nina did not resist.

5

It was amazing. One moment Skye Fargo was sore and stiff and would feel a sharp pang low on his ribs when he breathed deep. But the very instant that Nina Youngblood's lips met his, the soreness and stiffness melted away. The pangs were all but forgotten. Exquisite sensations rippled from his mouth downward. A warm, pleasant feeling came over him, as if he floated in a tub full of hot water. All of his fatigue evaporated like dew under the morning sun.

The kiss was incredible. Nina's lips were soft, pliant, deliciously sweet. They fit his perfectly. Immediately, they parted, and her silken tongue glided forth to entwine with his. He swirled it around and around, along her gums, the roof of her mouth, and out again to lick her mouth. She responded in kind.

Fargo's pole surged. He eased backward, then lowered her beside him. Nina stretched out so they were chin to chin, chest to breast, hip to thigh. He smelled the earthy scent of her hair. His mouth roved to her ear, where she had dabbed some perfume, and he sucked on her lobe. She was sensitive there, cooing and squirming while her hands played in his hair and probed his wide shoulders.

When Fargo raised his head to drink in her sensual beauty, she smiled invitingly and traced the outline of his chin with a tapered finger.

"Did you know I wanted you the minute we first met?"

"It took you that long?" Fargo quipped, his face dropping to hers. He feasted on her lips, devouring them in a kiss that was more than a kiss, a kiss that seared both of them to their cores and aroused flames of raw desire.

Nina was a bold vixen. While they sucked on each other's tongues, her hands roamed down his back to his buttocks and kneaded them as if they were bread dough. She liked to pinch and fondle.

Fargo kept his own hands busy. He parted her robe enough to admit his exploring fingers, which soon found a glorious mound at which to dally. Her nipple was erect and hard. When he tweaked it, she gasped and ground her hips against him. Apparently she was sensitive everywhere. Either that, or it had been some time since she had shared herself with a man. He cupped her and squeezed, eliciting a low cry she stifled by burying her face against his shoulder. When he lightly pulled on the nipple, she arched her spine like a she-cat and her fingernails dug into his flesh.

Fargo opened the robe more. His other hand descended to her other breast. At first contact, Nina flung her legs wide. She wanted him, craved him. But he was not in any rush. He would rather savor her as a fine wine should be savored. He would rather incite her passions inch by tantalizing inch.

They kissed many times, each hotter and wetter. His mouth lavished them on her smooth forehead, on her full cheeks, her flawless chin. His mouth nibbled a path ever lower until his face was between her globes. Which to choose? He clamped his lips on her left nipple, and sucked. It was enough to bring her up off the ground as if she were striving to take wing. Her arms wrapped tight around him, her legs stroked his from thigh to toe. She was not the type to lie there passive, letting him do all the work. She did her utmost to stoke his inner fires, as well.

Nina was a woman after Fargo's own heart. A woman who knew her own sexual appetites and was not afraid of them. A woman who did for the man everything the man did for her. She caressed his legs, his chest, then lowered a palm to his already throbbing manhood and rubbed it briskly. It was almost enough to make him explode, then and there. Gritting his teeth, he maintained control. Just barely.

Meanwhile, Fargo lathered her wonderful mounds, giving each rigid nipple the attention it deserved. She liked to have them massaged and flicked, so he did both for long minutes on end. Her hips began to sway, her legs to open and close.

Fargo undid her belt and the robe fell completely open, revealing her upper body in all its magnificent splendor. Her breasts were superb, full and ripe and curved upward at the tips, like fruit ready to burst. He enfolded each in his mouth in turn while squeezing them with his hands. Her breath grew hot enough to spark a paper into flame. Her whole body quivered and would not stop.

Fargo's lips dipped across the flat of her stomach to her navel. His tongue rimmed it, and she moaned. Lower still, and he nuzzled crinkly hairs sweetly scented. Then he was at the junction of her thighs, being overwhelmed by the heady fragrance of her womanhood. Her fingers glued themselves to his hair as he licked first one inner thigh and then the other. She was panting like a thoroughbred that had just won a race.

Ever so lightly, Fargo brushed his mouth across her warm slit. She was drenched with her own juices. His tongue slid out, along the fold, and Nina opened her mouth wide as if to scream. Inserting the tip into her tunnel, he tasted her salty, tangy nectar. When he rimmed her walls, she pushed his head inward. He licked and swirled, consuming her, unable to get enough. Soon she spurted, clamping her legs to his ears, her dainty bottom bouncing up off the blanket in regular cadence.

She wanted to make sounds. He could tell. But with the tent so near, she dared not. Several times she pressed a palm over her mouth to smoother an outcry. Several times she bit her lower lip for the same reason. Once, when his tongue delved deep up into her, she could not resist groaning. After that, she would turn her mouth to the saddle whenever she could not contain herself. An extreme measure, but it helped in that she did not utter any more loud noises.

The lower half of Fargo's face was slick with glistening love dew when he slowly glided his lips to her swollen knob. She trembled violently at the contact. Her eyes grew as wide as saucers. He proceeded to rub his tongue up and down, back and forth, over and over and over. Nina mewed like a kitten.

Fargo dallied forever. He would please her totally, then himself. To that end, he flicked and sucked and caressed until her body was practically vibrating like a guitar string, the melody he had inspired one of pure unbridled lust. Her hands stroked his hair, his shoulders, his upper arms. Her legs were clamped around him as if she would never let him go.

Presently, Fargo rose onto his knees. Unhitching his gunbelt and pants, he lowered both. As his member surged free, her hand enfolded it, her touch as light as a feather. It brought a lump to his throat. It was his turn to stiffen and gasp as her fingers delicately ran up and down the whole length.

"So big. So big," Nina whispered.

Fargo kneaded her breasts while she devoted herself to his organ. She acted fascinated by it. Her fingers went from top to bottom and back again. She would cup and squeeze, then work her hand higher or lower, squeezing every inch or so. She did this again and again. It felt so good, he never wanted her to stop. But she did, only to replace her hand with her mouth.

Now Fargo shivered. Now he squirmed. He struggled to hold himself in check while she did things that would cause most men to erupt in ecstasy. His fingers were in her soft hair as he rocked back and forth, so close to the brink, so very close.

The second that Nina lifted her head, Fargo pushed her flat, aligned the end of his pole with her tunnel, and rammed in to the hilt. The abruptness caught her off guard. She was heaved up off the blanket, her head thrown back, her lips formed in a delectable oval, like strawberries in their prime.

"Ohhhhhhh."

Fargo slammed into her repeatedly, forcefully. Her legs bent up and back. Her hands were on his sides. Nina rose to meet his thrusts, matching them, settling into a steady rhythm, her pelvis and his grinding in unison. Her inner walls were hotter than ever, rippling like waves in an ocean. In and almost out, in and almost out, he moved faster and faster and harder and harder.

Nina tossed her head from side to side, her eyelids fluttering. She moaned, adrift in the rapture of their joining. She was a volcano on the brink of eruption.

So was Fargo. He had held it in as long as he could. He must let it out, soon, whether she had reached the pinnacle or not. Then she rose up off the ground, looked deep into his eyes, and convulsed in ultimate joy. He felt her gush, felt her wetness coat him like a moist glove. It triggered his own release. Fargo came and came, driving up into her as if to cleave her in twain. Each second of time became an eternity of bliss. He was detached from himself, floating like a cloud, filled with pure elation. And he never wanted to come back down to earth.

But all good things come to an end and this was no exception. Fargo coasted to an exhausted stop. His whole body was caked with sweat. The chill breeze broke him out in goosebumps as he slumped on top of Nina. He rolled to the left so as not to burden her with his weight. She was completely still, barely breathing, eyes closed, her full mouth quirked upward, a portrait of true contentment.

"You were incredible," she whispered.

He returned the compliment, then rested his cheek on the saddle. Her own cheek fell onto his chest. Sluggish, tired, he tugged at the top blanket and covered them both. He did not mean to fall asleep but his body had a mind of its own. Slumber claimed them.

Fargo might well have slept until dawn except her snoring awoke him about an hour and a half later. Her mouth was next to his ear, and it sounded as if a bear were trying to rip into his skull. He shook her, gently. Nina smacked her lips but did not awaken. So he tried again, shaking both shoulders. All that did was get her to stop snoring.

She was dead to the world. It dawned on him that this might be the first good sleep she'd had since her father was murdered. He favored letting her stay with him through the night, but they ran the risk of discovery, either by Ella or, worse, by Mandy. It might shock the little girl, might upset her immensely. So, to spare the child, he gripped Nina's arms and pumped them several times. That did the trick.

Nina sat bolt upright, blinking and glancing in all directions. "What—?" she blurted in confusion.

Fargo pressed a finger to her soft lips. She realized where she was, smiled coyly, and impishly bit his skin. Just then the blanket slid off, exposing her charms. Clutching it, she pulled it up over her breasts and rotated so her back was to him. "Don't look," she whispered, closing her robe.

Fargo held back laughter. The antics of the opposite sex never ceased to amuse him. Here, they had just made love. He had seen all of her there was to see, touched her from her hair to her feet. Yet now she didn't want him to get a glimpse of her naked body. And she was not the first to act this way.

Many women Fargo met had done the same. He'd always figured it must be due to false modesty, a belief they had to act ladylike even when there was no need. Only recently had he come to view it in a new light. It wasn't an act. They weren't pretending. At heart, every woman really *was* a lady. While they might give in to passion when the mood was right, while they might do a hundred and one things they would never tell anyone, when their passion faded, when their ardor cooled, the lady inside of them came to the surface again and they were just as they had been before letting carnal hunger get the better of them.

Nina rose and twisted. "Thank you," she said softly. Then,

like a spooked doe, she bounded to the tent and ducked inside.

Grinning, Fargo adjusted his pants, strapped on his gunbelt, and lay back down. The fire had gone out. Enough starlight existed for him to distinguish the silhouettes of distant jagged peaks, shining white with snow. He pulled his hat brim low and made himself comfortable. In due course he was on the verge of dreamland.

The crunch of a twig brought Fargo fully awake again. He promptly rolled to the right, away from his saddle, snagging the Henry as he did. The horses were dozing, except for the Ovaro, which had pricked its ears and was staring to the east. He did likewise. He hoped it was an animal, a deer or an elk or even a bear that had wandered in from the forest. But the vague shape that shortly materialized moved on two legs, not four.

Fargo considered and discarded likely prospects. It wouldn't be an Indian for two reasons. First, Indians were seldom abroad at night. Some tribes believed that those who died in the dark would be unable to find their way to the next life. Other tribes were more practical. A warrior could not shoot what he could not see, and at night visibility was limited. The second reason had to do with the Utes. This was their territory. And while they were not currently at war with the white man, enough suspicion and ill will existed that no Ute who valued his hide would venture into a white encampment after sunset.

Could it be a prospector returning extra late from Dew Claw? Fargo had his doubts. Those who had gone had returned hours ago, conspicuous by their drunken swaggers and off-key singing.

Then might it simply be someone out for a stroll? Someone who could not sleep and was stretching his legs?

No, for whoever it was had tucked at the waist and was making a beeline for the Youngbloods' tent. In one hand was a long, slender object. A rifle. It had to be. In the other was a dully glinting blade.

Fargo fixed a bead on the man's midsection. Whoever it was, he was up to no good. The knife was for slitting the canvas. The rifle for killing whoever the man was after. And it was not hard to guess who that might be. Fargo had been there slightly over twenty-four hours, yet already he had more enemies than the Blackfeet.

The skulker was within ten feet of the tent and still Fargo could not see him clearly. Impressions were all Fargo had. Impressions of bulk and size. Of agility. It was a big man, light on his feet, like a cat. Making no more noise than would a ghost. If not for the accidental crunch of the twig, Fargo would never have known the would-be assassin was there.

Fargo would have given anything for a clear view of the man's face. He thought there was a beard but he could not be sure. The pants and shirt were dark enough to almost blend into the background. Slowly, so as not to result in a loud click, Fargo thumbed back the Henry's hammer.

The prowler had the ears of a cat, too. Halting, he spun, staring directly at the base of the cliff. In another heartbeat he had whirled and fled, a human antelope whose speed would be difficult to match.

Fargo gave chase anyway. He did not shoot. Snapping off a few shots might bring the man down, but stray bullets might strike sleeping prospectors. So he ran for all he was worth, never losing ground, never gaining any, either. Several times the man's face flashed white as he glanced over a shoulder.

Suddenly the skulker slanted toward Dead Cow Creek. Sprinting between a pair of tents, he vaulted a sluice trough and churned across a pool. The water rose as high as his knees, slowing him.

Fargo was close to the sluice when he saw his quarry pivot and jerk the rifle up. His only recourse was to dive flat. A rock gouged into his gut, another gashed his elbow. The blast he anticipated did not ring out. After several seconds he risked a peek to learn why.

It had been a ruse. The man had no intention of shooting. Not when gunfire would rouse the miners and bring them from their beds in a fury. No, the prowler had used the precious seconds Fargo had wasted to push on across the pool and was now almost to the other side. Cursing himself for being the biggest jackass in all Creation, Fargo flung himself up and over the sluice and hurtled into the creek. The water slowed him down just as it had the other. By the time he was in the middle, the human antelope was in the clear and flying up a slope to the crest of a hill.

There were no tents anywhere near. Nothing prevented Fargo from wedging the Hawken to his shoulder and firing. Except, when he did, the hammer fell on an empty chamber. He could have sworn he had levered a new round earlier.

"Damn!"

The man was almost to the top. Fargo had one last clear shot. In a fluid motion he fed a new cartridge in, whipped the stock high, and sighted down the barrel. He was a fraction too late. The skulker sped over the rim and was lost from sight.

Unwilling to give up, Fargo waded across and hastened toward the top. His wet soles slipped on loose stones, nearly spilling him. Scrambling fiercely, he clawed higher and higher until he could see over. A benighted gorge unfolded, as black as the pit, as silent as a grave. He did not stand up, for to do so would put him in the prowler's sights. Foiled, he crouched and mulled whether to sneak on around to the far side and try to flush the coyote out.

In the end, Fargo decided to go back. Running around blindly would only get him killed. He was better off waiting for daylight. Then he might learn something. Retracing his steps, he walked between the same two tents. Without warning a rifle muzzle was thrust at him.

"Hold up there, mister. Who the hell are you? And what's all the ruckus?"

The voice was familiar. "Barney Fiddlemeyer?"

"Fargo? That you?" The oldster stepped out clad only in

his long underwear. He did not lower his Sharps. "What in tarnation is going on? Don't you know any better than to go slinking around at this time of night? Are you trying to get yourself killed?"

Fargo explained, briefly.

"A big man, you say?" Fiddlemeyer scratched his bushy beard. "Well, that doesn't help much. Must be fifty men or better hereabouts who are as big or bigger than Harve Barclay." He leaned forward as if to confide a secret. "Between you and me, I wouldn't be surprised if it wasn't a young fellow come to call on one of the older Youngblood sisters. Those gals are wild as mustangs. If'n they're not mighty careful, they'll wind up shameless hussies parading their bodies for money." He warmed to his topic. "It's their pa's fault. Spare the rod and spoil the child. Were they mine, I'd tan their bottoms every day just for the hell of it, and twice on the Lord's day. Mark my words. They'd become proper ladies, or else!"

From within the second tent someone bellowed, "What the hell is all that jabbering about? Let a man sleep or there will be hell to pay."

"Go back to bed, Krimpton," Fiddlemeyer responded. To Fargo he said, "Maybe you should post a guard at their tent, just to be safe. I wouldn't mind standing watch. An old fella like me can go whole days without much sleep."

It was a sensible idea, but Fiddlemeyer was a bit too eager for Fargo's liking. He wouldn't put it past the old devil to steal into the sisters' tent and paddle their behinds while they were sleeping. Just to set them on the straight and narrow, of course. "No thanks. I can handle things."

"You sure? It wouldn't take me but a minute to get my britches on." Fiddlemeyer smiled crookedly. "You wouldn't have to worry none. I'd do for those girls like they were my own."

That's what Fargo was afraid of. "I'll keep your offer in mind," he said, and hurried off to forestall more chatter. From then on he gave every tent, shack, and lean-to a wide berth. Once at the cliff, he sat with his back against it, the Henry across his legs. It was unlikely the prowler would try again but he was not taking anything for granted. Draping a blanket over his shoulders, he permitted himself to fall into a light sleep. The slightest of noises awakened him. The stamp of a hoof. The swish of an owl's wings overhead. Even the chirp of a cricket.

Dawn came much too soon. A pink tinge framed the eastern horizon when Fargo sat up straight and stretched. Aches and pains plagued him again, especially where Guthrie had kicked him.

Casting off the blanket, Fargo shuffled to the creek, knelt, removed his hat, and plunged his face into the cold water. An icy spear tore through him. In the blink of an eye, he was wide awake. He uncoiled, shaking his head. Another dip made every nerve jangle. A third, and he almost felt like a new man. Splashing upstream heralded the beginning of a new day for a few early risers anxious to work their claims.

Fargo had saddled the stallion and was ready to leave before the Youngblood sisters awakened. He was set to fork leather when Ella came out, as beautiful as a rose, her hair neatly combed and clean clothes clinging to her lithe form.

"Where do you think you're going?"

"I have something to do. I'll be back in a bit."

Ella's smile was as tantalizing as her sister's. "Just so you're not running out on us. I'll have breakfast ready in half an hour."

"I'll be here."

Locating where the skulker had crossed Dead Cow Creek was child's play for someone with Fargo's talents. Thankfully, Barney Fiddlemeyer was not up yet. Fargo forded to the slope beyond. His tracks and those of the big man he had chased were as fresh as newly cut daisies. Exactly *how* big the man had been was impressed on him by the size of the footprints. He was taller than average himself, so his own tracks were larger than most. But the prints of the nocturnal stalker were longer than his by a good inch, wider by half that.

The trail led into the gorge just as a spectacular sunrise occurred. At the bottom the man had gone due east, sticking close to cover. In over a mile the gorge widened, then ended not far from the rutted excuse for a road that linked Dew Claw to the claims along Dead Cow Creek. A horse had been left tied to a pine. Once mounted, the prowler had ridden toward Dew Claw.

Fargo did not follow the tracks into the mining camp. It would serve no purpose since by now the whole population was out and about and most of the prints had probably been obliterated. But he had an important clue that pointed the finger of blame at none other than Rowdy Joe Guthrie. The badman had sent an underling to finish him off. That had to be it.

Leftover venison was being roasted on the griddle when Fargo reached the Youngblood claim.

Mandy squealed happily and rushed over to give him a hearty hug. "Where have you been? I was worried."

"Just giving my pinto some exercise," Fargo fibbed. It would not do to agitate her with the truth. But he did need to tell the older sisters just as soon as he had a moment in private with them.

Ella poked the meat with a fork. "After we eat, I'll take you to where our pa was killed. Nina and Mandy are going in to Cavendar's to pick up the supplies we need. We'll all meet back here at noon."

Fargo did not see any danger in the pair paying a visit to the mercantile. Even a cutthroat like Rowdy Joe would not dare harm a female, particularly a child. West of the Mississippi women were as rare as gemstones. Men put them on pedestals, treated them like they were queens. Any yack who violated one paid dearly. A man could carve another man into tiny pieces and no one would care, but let a woman be so much as touched improperly and the offender might have his neck stretched.

Nina avoided staring at him. Maybe she was embarrassed by what they had done. Maybe she regretted it. Women generally liked to have a man devote his heart and soul to them before they gave them their bodies. The only time she faced him was when she handed him a plate and could not avoid it. He smiled, but all it earned him was a downturn of her mouth.

Fargo did not bother to try and figure out why. Long ago he had learned that attempting to understand women was a lot like beating one's head against a tree. Both gave a man a headache, and both were pointless.

Ella hardly said two words while they ate, which was unusual for her. Mandy, though, bubbled over, saying how grand it was to have Fargo stay with them, and how she prayed he would stay a good long while. He did not break the bad news to her, yet.

Hitching the wagon took half an hour, only because one of the team balked at being put in harness. At last the deed was done, and Fargo and Ella stood and waved as the wagon clattered off. Mandy's arm flapped until she was lost amid the claims.

"Now it's just the two of us," Ella said with a mysterious grin. "I hope you're up to it."

They had to ride double. Fargo swung her up behind him and she sculpted herself to his back, her breath on the nape of his neck. As he brought the stallion to a trot, he could not help but wonder if the new day had as many surprises in store for him as the day before. If it did, he only asked one thing; to live through it.

6

"Here?"

"Yonder, in those trees," Ella Youngblood said. "I don't know how the man who found it did."

Skye Fargo wondered the same thing. Since her father had been on his way into Dew Claw when he vanished, Fargo had taken it for granted the blood-soaked piece of shirt had been found somewhere between Dead Cow Creek and the mining camp. That was not the case. Ella had guided him eastward beyond the last of the claims, then almost due south. In half a mile they came to a high knoll. And it was here Fargo had reined up and been informed that the spot they wanted was below in a stand of trees.

"Everyone was searching high and low," Ella continued. "I didn't count them, but there had to be over two hundred taking part. Even so, I reckon we were mighty lucky anything at all turned up."

Luck did not begin to describe it. Fargo glanced back. The main trail was not even visible from where they were. What had brought one of the searchers so far afield? Had there been tracks? Prints later wiped out by all those who came to see for themselves once word spread? "What was the name of the man who found it?"

Ella hesitated. "Mercy me. I just realized. I don't know who it was. A runner came to our tent and told us something had been found. He led Nina and me here while some friends kept watch over Mandy. By the time we arrived, there were sixty or seventy men milling around."

Which explained the confused jumble of footprints and hoofprints all over the knoll and down into the stand. Fargo kneed the pinto. It annoyed him that the prospectors had been so careless. Their excited tramping about had erased all clues as to the culprit's identity. No wonder the men who had hunted for sign had not found any.

"Nina was crying even before we got here," Ella revealed. "I think she sensed what had happened. I felt like bawling, too, but I refuse to cry in front of other people. Call it a quirk of mine, but I see it as being weak."

Fargo bent low to the ground. There were so many prints it was impossible to pick out any one set from another, whether man or beast.

Anxiety made Ella talkative. "I have this thing about being strong inside. Maybe it's because of how my mother always let Pa twist her around his little finger. Or the awful way she passed on. Or maybe it's just that I'll never give any man the satisfaction of seeing me act like a girl Mandy's age."

Fargo straightened and sighed. He might as well go into the trees although it would prove pointless.

The black-haired lovely misconstrued. "Why did you sigh? Don't you think women can be as strong as men? Don't tell me you're one of those who believes all females are somehow inferior just because they *are* female?"

Fargo thought no such thing, and said so. He'd met plenty of women who were independent and tough. One in particular stood out in his memory. A feisty muleskinner in Minnesota who could outfight and outdrink any male, a regular she-cat who had kowtowed to nobody.

"Glad to hear it," Ella said. "I don't think highly of men who believe women were put on this Earth for one reason and one reason alone."

Fargo did not ask what that reason was. He could guess. Winding in among the pines, he saw that the search party had trampled the undergrowth flat. "Where, exactly, was the piece of shirt found?"

Ella pointed straight ahead. "Just a little further." Her hands

75

rested on his shoulders, her fingers tense. She was extremely upset but doing her best not to show it. "For the life of me, I can't imagine why Pa would come here on his own. Whoever murdered him must have made him do it. At gunpoint, I bet."

Possibly, Fargo mused. The stand was well off the beaten path. Safe enough for a killer to dispose of his victim. But that beggared a critical question. What had happened to Brian Youngblood's *body*?

As if Ella could read his mind, she commented, "One thing I don't savvy is where my pa's body got to. No grave was found. No piles of brush or limbs were found with it underneath. It just up and vanished."

"What about his personal belongings? His pistol? His knife?"

"Pa didn't own a belly gun. He had his new rifle with him that day, a Spencer." Anguish laced Ella's voice. "None of his other effects ever turned up. I know he never went anywhere without his Green River knife. And he always carried a leather poke that hung from his belt. In it he kept a necklace of Ma's and some other keepsakes." Her fingers gouged deeper. "Hold up. This is it."

They had reached a clearing ten feet in diameter. Encircled by trees, it could not be seen until someone was right on top of it. Fargo slid off the stallion and examined the soil. Not that there was anything worth the effort. A multitude of feet had churned the grass into a shambles. Except in the very center where a cluster of stems stood undisturbed. Closer inspection showed why. A few still bore telltale dull crimson streaks. "This is where the piece was found."

Ella had climbed down. She nodded, her gaze elsewhere.

"Nothing else?"

"No."

"Nothing at all?"

Exasperated, she gestured testily, still refusing to look at the stains. "How many times must I tell you? Just that part of his shirt."

"Did anyone come across any blood elsewhere?"

"Not a drop."

Rising, Fargo moved in ever-widening circles. He was more perplexed than ever. If this was indeed where Brian Youngblood had been slain, there should be more to go by. The shirt had been soaked through and through, hinting at a wound that punctured a vein. Blood would have gushed like a geyser. Even if the killer had dragged the body off, or thrown Youngblood over a horse, blood would have gotten all over the place.

Fargo entered the trees. Circle after circle took him farther and farther from the clearing. Ella followed, but she was not interested in what he was doing. Chin hung low, she was lost in sorrow. Only after they were out of the stand did she stir and regard him with curiosity.

"Mind explaining what you're up to? What do you hope to find that scores of other men couldn't?"

"I can't rightly say," Fargo conceded. Rotating a full three hundred and sixty degrees, he scrutinized the nearby slopes and woodland. To the southeast a couple of hundred yards reared a rock outcropping the size of a log cabin. He faced the stand and whistled shrilly. Within moments the Ovaro was there.

"He sure is well trained," Ella mentioned.

Fargo climbed on, offered his hand. At a trot they rode to the outcropping. It was horseshoe-shaped, the open end in the direction of Dew Claw and not apparent from the stand.

Swinging down, Fargo inspected the barren tract the outcropping ringed. Hoofprints told him a single horse had been tethered there for a short while quite some time ago. About two weeks previous would be his guess. Coincidence? He doubted it.

Ella was glued to his heels. "Tracks! How did you know they would be here?"

"I didn't."

"It was just one rider? What was he doing? Spying on the search party?"

Fargo pointed at several partial footprints. The impressions were faint because the ground was so hard. Not much could be gleaned from them. But it was plain the rider had dismounted and gone on around the outcropping, toward the stand.

"Any idea who it might have been? Or what he was doing?" Ella asked. "It couldn't have been one of the searchers. Why would an Argonaut hide his horse?"

The term "Argonaut" was a reference to the old tale about Jason and the Argonauts, who set sail from ancient Greece in their ship, the *Argo*, on a fabled quest for the Golden Fleece. It became popular during the California rush of '49. A journalist had written an account of the gold-hungry legions trekking westward in search of fortune and fame, "just like the Argonauts of antiquity who braved the unknown perils of the sea." The name had stuck.

"It makes no darn sense," Ella remarked.

Fargo was stumped, too. He noticed that the rider had returned, then gone off in the direction of Dew Claw. Exactly *when* was the big question. Had it been before the blood-stained material was found? Afterward? Or while all the prospectors were combing the vicinity? He climbed onto the outcropping for a better view of the countryside.

Ella had her arms clasped to her chest. "This whole mess is one giant mystery. I'm beginning to think no one can unravel it." She fluttered her lips in vexation. "I wish to hell my pa had never brought us here. I wish we were still living in Ohio, and Ma was still alive. I wish—".

Movement to the north alerted Fargo to the fact they were not alone. Spotting the source, he jumped down, dashed to Ella, and placed a hand over her mouth. Reacting on instinct, she started to pull loose, desisting when he whispered urgently in her ear. "Hush! We've got company."

Her eyes mirrored the question she could not speak aloud.

Fargo moved closer to the outcropping, then pointed. Two horsemen had appeared near the stand, moving around it from north to south. Both had rifles in their hands. And both had the unmistakable stamp of killers-for-hire.

"More of Guthrie's bunch!" Ella whispered when he lowered his arm. "I've seen them in Dew Claw. That one in the sombrero is a Mexican called Julio. He's real quiet but real deadly, they say. The other man is known as Lash Larson. He got uppity with Nina once and she slapped him."

Fargo moved to the stallion. Were he alone, he would stay and fight. But he had Ella to think of. Forking leather, he pulled her up one more time. "Stay low. If I tell you to jump, jump."

"Jump off while we're moving?" she responded in disbelief. "Why on earth would I want to do that?"

Careful to keep the outcropping between them and the gunmen, Fargo clucked to the pinto. The hardcases were bound to spot its tracks and investigate. He had to cover as much ground as he could before then.

Rowdy Joe Guthrie certainly was persistent. The man Guthrie sent last night had failed so now two more had been given the job. Fargo was almost sorry he had put off confronting Guthrie in order to heal up. Indirectly, it had put Ella's life in danger.

"Maybe we should head for Dew Claw," she suggested.

Fargo had already discarded the notion as too risky. Guthrie would have men on the lookout. As soon as he got there, they would swarm over him like hornets. He might be able to hold his own alone. But not when he was hindered by having to protect Ella; he couldn't watch her back and his at the same time.

"Enough is enough," she was saying. "We can't keep living like this. Always afraid. Never knowing when one of these varmints might show up. Might ride into our camp like Mundy and his friends did. After we lose these two, I'm going to go into Dew Claw and brace Rowdy Joe myself."

Fargo believed she would. "You'll do no such thing."

"Who's going to stop me? No offense, but you're not my pa. Or my husband. So you have no say in the matter. I'm a grown woman and can do as I damn well please."

"Let me take care of him."

"Rowdy Joe isn't going to go easy on you like he did the other day. He has to make wolf meat of you for what you did to Mundy and Rickert. He has to prove to everyone that no one bucks him and lives. That's why he sent these new fellers." Ella twisted to look to the west. "Five dollars says they were on their way to Dead Cow Creek and saw us leave the trail." She swore. "We've played right into their hands. There are no witnesses about. They can kill us with no one the wiser."

"They can try," Fargo said. He was making for a finger of forest that bordered a hill strewn with boulders. Once they were under cover, let the gunmen come. He would pick them off and send them back to their boss draped over their saddles. Half the population of Dew Claw would see their mounts arrive. Word would spread. Guthrie's hold on the Argonauts would weaken. It would be the beginning of the end for the criminal element.

Or would it? There was always Luke Olinger. Of the two, he was smarter. And that made him deadlier. But would he lift a finger to help Rowdy Joe? No love was lost between them. Olinger had let it drop they were business partners, though in what regard was unknown.

Suddenly Fargo remembered something else. A comment Guthrie had made while mashing his face into the mud. "I should kill you right here and now. Snap your back like a dry twig. But we're not supposed to kill anyone unless we get permission first." What in the world did that mean? Permission from whom? And who was the "we" Guthrie referred to? Olinger and him? If not, there had to be a third "partner," a person no one else knew anything about, someone who pulled the strings of both men as if they were puppets. "Does Guthrie have any acquaintances you know of besides Luke Olinger?"

"Just the gun sharks who work for him," Ella said. "Most everyone else hates his guts. Months ago there was talk of appointing a marshal to run Joe and his boys off, but nothing ever came of it. The Council said whoever pinned on the star wouldn't have much legal standing. So the idea was dropped." She snorted. "But I don't think that was the real reason. Rumor has it they couldn't find anyone brave enough to wear the tin."

"What Council?" Fargo asked.

"Sorry. You wouldn't know. The Dew Claw Betterment Council. Closest thing to a town council Dew Claw has. It's made up of all the top businessmen. Men like Olinger and Lester Cavendar and eight or nine others. Oh. And the minister. Reverend Percy. He's the one who came up with the idea."

"Olinger must have been mad enough to spit tacks."

"Funny thing, there," Ella said. "I heard there was a vote, and it was unanimous. Olinger voted with the rest to hire a marshal if one could be found. Now why would he do that? Given that Guthrie and him are in cahoots?"

Fargo shrugged. The more he learned, the more puzzled he became. Had Olinger done it as a lark? Or just to go along with the others? Olinger was savvy enough to realize that agreeing to the proposal was one thing, being able to carry it out quite another.

"I'd have worn that badge for them," Ella declared. "But perish forbid they should ask a woman to do a man's job. Why, the world might come to an end."

They were halfway to the forest. Fargo was so deep in thought, he neglected to keep watch to their rear. So when Ella cried out, he was taken aback to see that Julio and Lash had passed the rock outcropping and broken into a gallop. The pair were in rifle range and had a clear shot. But strangely enough, neither cut loose.

Not one to quibble over miracles, Fargo lashed the stallion and raced for cover. He yanked on the Henry and it popped from the scabbard as if the inside were coated with bear fat. The moment he twisted and brought the rifle up, Julio and Lash slowed and separated, one angling to the right, the other to the left. The Mexican swung onto the offside of his mount, Comanche style.

"Why didn't they shoot?"

Fargo had no idea. He had pointed the Henry at them. What more of an excuse did they need? He sped on into the woods and through the belt of vegetation to the bottom of the hill. Julio and Lash were still back there, crashing through the brush in their haste to catch up. Spurring the Ovaro up the slope, he reined into the shadow of a boulder large enough to shield it from flying lead. "Stay right where you are."

"What are you up to?" Ella asked.

Fargo vaulted off and sprinted down the slope to a smaller, shoulder-high slab with a flat top. Placing the Henry on it, he took a step back, then hurtled upward. His elbows cleared the rim and he wedged them fast, using them for leverage as he wriggled upward until he was prone. Lying still, he raked the tree line.

The gunmen were quick to show themselves. Reunited, they climbed side-by-side, their rifles held across their saddles rather than ready to fire. A bullwhip was looped around Lash's saddle horn, which explained his nickname. Julio was the first to halt when Fargo rose with the Henry leveled.

"That's far enough."

Drawing rein, the hardcases obeyed. Neither man jerked his rifle into play. Julio's mustache straightened in a smile. Lash just sat there, unruffled.

"Why are you trailing us?" Fargo demanded.

Julio chuckled. "Maybe, hombre, we are out for—how you say—a breath of fresh air, eh? A ride in the sun."

"I know you work for Rowdy Joe."

Lash winked at the Mexican. "We've got us a smart one here, pard. He'd put a tree full of owls to shame." Snickering, he glanced up. "Hell, mister. We've been doggin' you for over an hour. If we'd wanted to fill you and the pretty missy full of holes, we'd have done it long before this."

Fargo almost believed him. They were remarkably calm about being caught. But only a raving idiot would take them at their word. "Drop your rifles."

"And get them all scratched up?" Lash protested. "Can't we just shove 'em back in their scabbards? I give my range word we won't try to put windows in your skull."

"Drop them."

"Damn. You're a contrary cuss." Lash glared but complied, partly. Instead of letting his rifle fall, he slowly lowered it by the tip of the barrel until it rested gently on the ground.

Julio leaned down, letting his fall onto a patch of grass. "If it is damaged, *senor*, you will buy Julio a new one. This Julio promises you."

Fargo rose. No other short-trigger men were anywhere in sight. "Now shuck your revolvers."

Lash hissed like a cottonmouth. "This is gettin' downright ridiculous. How many times do I have to tell you? We could have rubbed you out any time we wanted. That we didn't should prove we're not out to do you harm."

The Mexican made a show of opening his hand wide and pulling his ivory-handled Colt with two fingers. "Do as he wants, *amigo*. We have our orders. And don't hold it against him. A man can never be too cautious, eh?"

Lash vented a string of lusty curses, but he drew his pistol and hung from the saddle horn to set it on the ground. The scowl he bestowed on Fargo as he straightened would wilt a plant. "What's next, damn you? Want us to shuck our clothes? Or maybe you'd like to take our horses and make us walk all the way back to Dew Claw?"

Julio tilted his sombrero. "Don't give him any ideas. This *hombre* might just do it. He is a hard one, Julio thinks."

"So am I, and I don't like this one bit," Lash grated, not appeased. "It galls me, Guthrie or no Guthrie. No man has ever made me eat crow before."

"All he does is make sure we can not shoot him. What is so wrong with that, *amigo*? We would do the same."

Fargo had never met their like. He was holding a rifle on them, and they squabbled like a couple of children. "Mind if I interrupt?" he asked. "Suppose you tell me why you've been shadowing us. Rowdy Joe sent you?"

Lash folded his hands on top of his saddle horn. "You must be one of them there geniuses people talk about. Who else would it have been? He wants to see you. To talk."

"*Sí, senor*," Julio said. "Only to parley."

Fargo was skeptical. Guthrie did not strike him as the forgiving sort. "Why? What does he want to talk about?"

"How the devil would we know?" Lash retorted. "He doesn't take us into his confidence. We're hired help, is all. He says to do somethin' and we do it." The dour gunman ran a hand over stubble on his jaw. "Joe told us to fetch you, mister. Made it clear we weren't to lay a finger on you or we'd answer to him. That's the whole story."

Were they telling the truth? Unlikely as it was, Fargo could think of no other explanation for how these two had behaved. Against his better judgment he lowered the Henry. "Where does he want to meet?"

"Where else? The Timberline," Lash said. He snapped his fingers as if he had recalled something important. "Almost forgot. He guarantees you safe conduct, into Dew Claw and out again. His very words. Just in case you suspect he has some of the other boys lyin' in ambush."

"Is Olinger involved in this?"

Lash exhaled loudly. "Your ears must be plugged with wax. If Joe don't tell us diddly, what makes you think Luke would? He's not one to suffer from diarrhea of the jawbone."

Julio gestured. "We are sorry, *senor*. But only Rowdy Joe can answer your questions. *Por favor*. Come with us, eh? You have taken our guns. What can we do?"

"I wouldn't trust them, Skye." From around the base of the flat-topped rock came Ella Youngblood, her revolver out. Without being told, she began to collect their hardware. "From the stories I've heard, these two are the worst of the pack. They're wanted down in Texas for killing a rancher and his four sons."

Lash's mouth twitched. "Well, well. Look who it is. Charmed life herself."

Ella paused. "How's that?"

It was Julio who answered. "No one is to hurt you, *senorita*. Ever. You or your *hermanas*. Your sisters."

"On whose say-so?" Ella quizzed him.

"The top man himself," Lash replied.

"Which one is that? Olinger or Guthrie?"

For a moment Fargo thought one of them would tell her. But the blond man and the Mexican only laughed. "Maybe you should ask Rowdy Joe next time you see him," Lash suggested. "Or better yet, Olinger. He has a weakness for the ladies. A lovely filly like you will make him melt. Wouldn't surprise me if he babbled like a brook."

Ella had Julio's guns and was backing up. She placed them well out of their reach, then moved to claim Lash's. The hardcases made no attempt to stop her. "I want to see both, to learn which one of those bastards had my pa killed."

"Julio is sorry, *senorita*," Julio said, "but only this one"— he nodded at Fargo—"is to go with us. You must go back to your claim. Stay with your sisters. In time you will have the answers you want, I think."

"Shut up," Lash said harshly.

Ella stopped between their horses. "What did you say that for?" she asked the Mexican. "Who is going to supply them?"

Lash grinned crookedly. "Sometimes Julio runs off at the mouth. I thought of sewin' it shut but then he'd starve to death and I wouldn't have anyone to darn my socks."

Fargo was tired of their nonsense. He had come to a decision, so he stepped to the edge of the slab. "I'll take Miss Youngblood back, then meet you outside of Dew Claw. It shouldn't take more than an hour."

"Whatever you want, *senor*," Julio said, his arms dangling. He lifted a leg to scratch below the knee, then suddenly turned his wrist sharply and a small knife was in his palm. He had it pressed against Ella's throat before she had any idea what he had done. "Do not twitch, *senorita!*"

Fargo began to sweep the Henry up. He had been duped. The pair had been as slick as axle grease. A signal had been exchanged unnoticed, because even as he brought the rifle to bear, the end of Lash's bullwhip flashed toward him.

7

Lash Larson was aptly named. His skill with a bullwhip was extraordinary, as he demonstrated by flicking it up and out as fast as a striking rattler. It wrapped around the barrel of Skye Fargo's rifle just as Fargo squeezed the trigger, and Lash wrenched hard. The Henry was torn from Fargo's grasp, the slug intended for Larson thudding into the dirt near his mount and kicking up a spray of dust.

Instantly, Fargo stabbed for his Colt.

Julio had hold of Ella's hair. "Don't even think it, *senor!*" he warned. "Not if you value the *senorita's* life."

Fargo froze. The *pistolero's* blade was gouging into her throat. Another fraction, and it would draw blood. He flung both arms out from his sides to show he would not endanger her life. Lash's cold laughter bit into him like the teeth of a cougar.

"That's a good little fella. Now unbuckle your gunbelt and let it drop. Try anything, and my pard will slit that bitch from ear to ear. Savvy?"

Nodding once, Fargo did as he had been instructed, then elevated his hands. He was perched on the rim of the boulder. If the Mexican lowered the knife, he would leap and bowl Julio over, allowing Ella to seek safety. To distract the two killers, he commented, "I thought you said she isn't to be harmed."

"She is not supposed to be, no," Julio responded, dark eyes sparkling. "But accidents happen, eh? We will hide her body, then say you shot her by mistake. The big man will believe us."

"As for *you*," Lash said, slowly pulling the long length of braided rawhide toward him. "Hop on down here. I aim to have me some fun."

Julio glanced at his companion. "No. *Por favor, amigo.* Let us do as we came to do. Pick up your *pistola* and shoot him so we can be done with it."

Lash frowned. "Anyone ever tell you what a spoilsport you can be, pard? Why not indulge ourselves? You know how I love to play with the jackasses we kill before we turn them into maggot bait."

Fargo did not take his eyes off Julio's knife hand. The fingers had not relaxed a smidgen. Stalling for time, he remarked, "So you planned to kill me all along?"

"Of course." Lash chortled. "But we're smarter than Mundy. The fool! Ridin' right up to you like he did! He should have just shot you in the back." Lash reined his horse to the left a few yards, the whip slithering along the ground like a fifteen-foot snake. "Julio and me use our heads. We'd rather outwit someone than have to outdraw them."

"So everything you told me was a lie?"

"Not everything, exactly," Lash said. "But most of it. That business about Rowdy Joe wantin' to talk. About the safe conduct. All that was bull. We aimed to strap you bellydown on your pinto all along."

"I've got to hand it to you," Fargo said, edging a bit further out. He was balanced on the balls of his feet, his legs tensed to spring. "You had me completely fooled."

"Of course we did." Lash was immensely pleased with himself. "By the time I was seven years old I could lie with a straight face and my folks would swear on a stack of Bibles I was tellin' the truth. The idiots." His eyes narrowed. "I told you to jump down. I won't say it again."

Fargo stayed put. Once down there he would be at their mercy. He racked his brain for a way to induce Julio to release Ella. She had dropped her revolver and was staring up at him, eloquent appeal etched in her lovely features. Sneering scornfully, he said, "I didn't fall out of an apple tree an hour ago. You say that you like to use your heads. I say that's another lie. The truth is, you're both yellow."

Lash's right arm went rigid. "Be real careful, mister."

"Julio does not like to be insulted, *hombre*."

Fargo nodded at the Mexican. "Look at you. Hiding behind a woman." He nodded at Larson. "And you're no different. You trick people into letting their guard down because you're afraid to go up against them in a fair fight. If that isn't the mark of a coward, I don't know what is." Fargo saw Julio's knife hand begin to drop and he was on the verge of springing when the bullwhip sizzled like frying bacon. He felt the rawhide wrap around his lower legs, felt his feet yanked out from under him. Ella called his name. Then he struck, on his side, his arm and ribs flaring with torment. He missed being impaled on a sharp rock by mere inches.

Lash Larson wore fury like a veil. "You heard him, pard. No one can talk to me like that. I'm going to peel his skin from him a patch at a time."

Julio had finally taken the blade from Ella's throat. "Indulge yourself, *amigo*. All I ask is that you give him five or ten lashes for me."

"Oh, I'll give him a lot more than that." Larson's arm moved, and the bullwhip unwound from Fargo's legs as if it were a living thing. Lash's arm moved again, and the whip cracked in the air above Fargo's head. Cracked as loud as a gunshot. "On your feet, mister. We'll see how damn brave you are once I start whittlin' you down to size."

In the hands of an expert a bullwhip was as lethal as a gun. It was capable of ripping a man wide open, of shearing into flesh like a sharp knife into soft fruit, of taking out an eye with a flick. Fargo had seen mule skinners who could kill a fly on the wing. He watched the lash as he rose.

"Now run," Larson said, nodding at the slope. "Let's see how far you get."

Fargo glanced at Ella. She was scared, but more for his sake than for her own. "Don't worry," he said.

Inexplicably, it incensed Lash. The whip whizzed outward,

the rawhide biting into Fargo's forearm, clean through the buckskin and skin. "I told you to run, damn it!" He drew back the short wooden handle.

Agony speared Fargo from wrist to shoulder as he reluctantly jogged past their horses. He did not expect Lash to give him much of a head start, and he was right. Five seconds later Larson yipped for joy and wheeled the buttermilk. Spurs gleamed in the sunlight. The animal thundered in pursuit.

Fargo increased his speed. Avoiding a boulder, he leaped over a smaller one. Every few steps he glanced back. Lash was grinning wickedly. Fargo ducked as the rawhide sought the back of his head. It buzzed above him, clipping his hat. Doubling at the waist, he ran around another boulder, then angled to the left. He had an ace in the hole, but he did not want to use it where Julio would see.

Lash was enjoying himself. He deliberately held his animal to a brisk walk, toying with Fargo as a cat would a mouse. Again and again he blistered the air with the end of the whip, always coming close but not making contact. "Run, mister, run! Show us how much grit *you* have!"

Fargo put another large boulder behind him. Bending at the knees, he darted up the hill instead of down. A wide cleft in a column of stone was a godsend. Diving into it, he flattened. The clomp of hooves came closer, then stopped.

Larson uttered enough swear words to turn a river rat's ears blue.

"What is the matter, *amigo*?" Julio hollered.

"He gave me the slip," Lash said. "But don't fret. He's got to be here somewhere, hidin' like the rabbit he is."

Shod hooves rang on rock. A shadow fell across the cleft. Fargo glimpsed the buttermilk's nose.

"Where the hell are you, rabbit?" Lash taunted. "Quiverin' in your boots, I reckon. And I don't blame you. Because you know why? I'm going to blind you. Pop those eyes of yours like they were grapes."

The buttermilk's whole head appeared. Fargo hoped the animal would not do anything to give him away, but it did.

It looked right at the cleft and nickered. Surging into the clear, Fargo ducked just in time to avoid the rawhide. He ran flat out, weaving among the boulders to make it hard for Larson to connect. Again and again his ears were nearly sizzled by the burning lash. The killer continued to play with him. Which was fine by Fargo. Let Larson think he was helpless. The cutthroat would learn differently soon enough.

"Look at you run! I reckon you're not so cocksure of yourself now, are you, mister? Or should I call you 'bunny'?"

Fargo didn't answer. He had another ten yards to go before he would be high enough. A prickly bush barred his path and he had to bear to the right. It slowed him just enough for the whip to catch him across the shoulders. Again his buckskin shirt was sliced through as if it were thin paper. A warm, sticky sensation spread down his back.

"Ha! The bunny is bleedin'!" Lash hooted. "Julio, you should come see this. You're missin' the frolic."

"Just do not take all day!" the Mexican shouted.

Lash cackled. "You're worse than a blamed mother hen. Hold your britches on. I'll be there directly."

Fargo pumped his legs. He saw Larson's arm bend and threw himself at the ground. When nothing happened, he shifted. Lash had only pretended to swing, but now he did so in earnest. Fargo rolled, paying no heed to the scrapes and bruises he sustained. They were minor compared to the excruciating hurt of the whip when it cut deep into his left shoulder. Pushing erect, he bolted higher.

"A piece at a time, just like I promised!" Lash yelled. "Next it's one of your eyes, then the other."

More boulders loomed, providing temporary safety. Fargo counted the strides he took. Seven, eight, nine. A flat shelf no wider than his hips was ideal for what he had in mind. Turning at bay, he crouched, Lash was coming through the boulders. Off to the right, out of sight were Julio and Ella. "I'm done running. If you want me so much, come and get me."

Lash obliged by slapping his legs against the buttermilk. Wearing that evil grin of his, he charged up the incline. And when he was close enough, he swung the whip, crack-crack-crack, one swing right after the other, blistering the air—and Fargo.

The rawhide was a fluid sword, hacking into Fargo's arms, into his shoulders, into his chest. His hat was sent sailing. He sidestepped to the left, bringing both arms up to protect his head and face, It was not enough. He winced when the whip took a patch of hair and skin from above his ear. Another blow opened his scalp. One of the knuckles on his left hand was cracked like a walnut shell.

"What's the matter, rabbit?" Lash said, his arm flailing, flailing, flailing. "Scared of losing your tongue if you open your mouth?"

Fargo backed off, absorbing blow after punishing blow. His shirt was being ripped to tatters. His shoulders and head stung terribly from a dozen wounds. He did not whirl and run, as anyone else would have done. Suddenly he seemed to stumble, and sank onto his right knee.

The buttermilk reached the shelf. Lash stopped swinging, his chest heaving from his exertion. "Give up already?" he said. "Why is it the ones who talk tough are always such pussy kittens?"

Bent low as if in the worst agony, Fargo slid his right hand to the top of his boot. Strapped to an ankle sheath was his Arkansas toothpick, a slender knife almost as popular on the frontier as the Bowie. Unlike its famous cousin, the toothpick had a double-edged blade and tapered to a wedge-shaped point. His was perfectly balanced for throwing, and he had spent more hours than he cared to count doing just that. Often, when he stopped for the night, he would select a convenient target, usually a stump or a log, and throw until his shoulder was too sore to continue.

"Well, you lasted longer than most, if that makes you feel any better," Lash declared. "The last man I whipped to death keeled over after three swings. His heart gave out, I reckon." He wagged the wooden stock. "Bet you'd never guess I made my livin' as a mule skinner when I was younger."

Fargo palmed the toothpick. Raising his head, he said, "Are you fixing to talk me to death?"

Larson snarled like a panther. "Think you're clever, don't you? Mister, you can't hold a candle to Julio and me. You're the fourteenth pilgrim we've put into the grave since we paired up." He nudged the buttermilk nearer. "I killed a duck when I was seven, and I've been killin' ever since. It's in my blood, you might say. Me, I'm good at killin'. And know what? I like what I do."

"I never would have guessed," Fargo said, rising halfway, his right arm against his leg.

"Any last words before I turn your face to mush?"

"A few." Fargo took a short step to the right so the angle was more to his liking. "I remember what a Sioux warrior told me once, long ago. I was living with them at the time—"

Lash snickered. "I knew you were a filthy injun lover."

Fargo did not let it fluster him. "—and one day a war party went off to punish the Crows for a raid on the Minneconjou. It was led by Buffalo Hump, one of the best warriors in the whole tribe. He had counted over twenty coup. He was leader of the Fox Society. Yet when the war party came back, they carried his body. A Crow had killed him."

"So what's your point?" Lash snapped. "Injuns kill injuns all the time. Who the hell cares? The less gnats around, the fewer we have to kill ourselves."

"I'm getting to my point," Fargo said. Larson was hooked, despite himself. "I remember staring at Buffalo Hump's body. Next to me was an older warrior, Makes-Room. I asked him how it was that someone who had killed so many enemies had fallen to the Crows."

"Get your stupid yarn over with so I can finish this. My pard is waitin'."

"Makes-Room told me something I've never forgotten," Fargo related. His arm was loose, relaxed. He was as ready as he would ever be. "He said that no matter how good a man is at killing—" On purpose, Fargo stopped.

"What? What did he say? I want to know."

"No matter how good a man is at killing," Fargo repeated, "there is always someone, somewhere, who is better." He arced his hand up and around before the last word was out of his mouth. Sunlight glittered on polished metal. The razor-sharp blade penetrated to the hilt at the base of the badman's throat.

Lash Larson was starting to swing the bullwhip. Amazement turned him to marble. Then he sputtered and wheezed, spitting scarlet as he let go and grabbed the toothpick's hilt. Gurgling grunts issued from his mouth. He tugged with all his might. The blade came out, but so did a red torrent. "No!" he managed to squeak before his throat flooded with blood. He swiveled and threw his head back to bawl for help.

Fargo had other ideas.

Lunging, he seized hold of Larson's leg and propelled it upward. The killer toppled from the saddle and tumbled down the slope, coming to rest against a boulder. Lash tried to sit up, a red finger pointing at Fargo as if the gunman were scolding, "Shame on you!" Groaning, he slumped onto his back and gaped at clouds scuttling by. His lips moved but the sounds he made were more like the pathetic whimpering of a fatally stricken dog than those of a human being.

Fargo left the bullwhip where it had dropped. All he wanted was the toothpick. Wiping it clean on the back of his pants, he grasped the buttermilk's reins and headed for where he had left Ella and the Mexican.

Lash was not dead yet. Frothing at the mouth, he pushed himself up on one arm. "Bas—!" he spewed, but whatever else he was going to say was lost to posterity when a convulsion contorted him. He flopped like a fish out of water, a fish who expired with its mouth horribly agape.

"*Amigo!*" Julio shouted. "What's going on, eh? What was that noise I just heard? Did you finish him?"

Fargo ran, angling toward the voice. The buttermilk was as tame as a lamb and did exactly as he wanted, even when he slapped it on the rump.

"Lash? Is that you?"

Julio and Ella were only twenty or thirty feet away but Fargo could not see them. Loping to the right, he circled to approach them from behind. If all went well, the riderless buttermilk would keep Julio occupied the few seconds it would take to get into position.

"*Amigo*, why don't you an—" the Mexican began. His abrupt silence was proof he had seen his friend's horse.

Fargo had to move swiftly. Out of sheer spite, Julio might slay Ella. He crept around another slab, cat-footed past an oval boulder. He was turning to the left when he heard a thump and a low cry. A few long bounds and he beheld Ella on her back, Julio rearing above her, knife on high.

"Try me instead," Fargo said, and sprang. The gunman met his slash with a parry. Steel rang on steel. A thrust was blocked. A stab evaded. They circled one another, Julio holding his knife down low for a groin or a stomach slash.

"My compliments, *hombre*. You are almost as skilled as Julio. Almost, but not quite. Your end will come soon."

That remained to be seen. Fargo weaved the toothpick in a gleaming tapestry that would have penetrated the guard of most men. But not Julio. The cutthroat was true to his boast. Every tactic Fargo tried, Julio countered. Neither could break down the other. They parted again, both breathing heavily, Fargo with blood matting his hair and cheek from wounds inflicted by Lash's bullwhip.

"You are most *excelente, senor*," Julio said between breaths. "But you grow weaker, and Julio is as strong as ever." He stepped back a few feet to glance up the hill. "Tell me, *por favor*. Before we end this. My friend. He is dead, eh?"

"I wouldn't be alive if he weren't."

"Ah. He always was too headstrong, that one. He would never listen to Julio. He always thought he knew best."

Fargo looked at Ella. She had moved to one side, against a boulder and was gingerly rubbing a nasty welt on her forehead where she had been struck. Otherwise, she was unhurt. "Doesn't everyone?"

"*Senor?*"

"How would you like to ride out of here? Just mount up and go?"

Julio wiped a sleeve across his damp forehead. "What is the catch, as you *gringos* like to say?"

"There are two. Forget about Guthrie. Ride anywhere you want, but not to Dew Claw. Never show your face in these parts again."

"The second condition?"

"I want to know the name of the man who runs things. Is it Rowdy Joe? Luke Olinger? Or someone else?" The name was important. So important, Fargo was willing to let Julio live. Once Fargo knew who it was, he could put an end to the threat the man posed. Chop off the head of a serpent and the body died. The sisters would be safe. The gold hounds could get on with their lives.

"Julio wishes he could say."

"It's that, or an early grave," Fargo moved in again, the toothpick at his waist. "Which will it be?"

"Were it not for the pledge Julio made, he would tell you. But all of us promised to keep his name secret. It was one of *his* conditions. Had we refused, he would not have shown us how it was done."

"Who? How what was done?"

Julio raised his blade. "Think what you will of Julio, but he never breaks his word. So we fight on, *hombre*. And may *el Diablo* greet the loser in sheets of flame this day."

Fargo thought he was braced for the *pistolero's* onslaught but he was wrong. Julio waded into him like a man gone berserk. Their knives clanged, rasped, scraped. Fargo was cut on the side, not deep enough to need stitches but it still stung worse than a dozen bee stings. At the same moment, he sliced open the back of Julio's hand.

Without a break in stride, Julio was on him again, keeping Fargo on the defensive much more than he should be. Fargo had to change that. In a fight, the one who could not press an enemy hard was the one who fell to that enemy.

Fargo sidestepped, then speared the toothpick at Julio's

heart. Julio twisted just enough for the blade to miss him while he slashed at Fargo's wrist. A pivot, and Fargo met steel with steel. Julio growled, much like a wolverine, and like a wolverine he closed in swift and low, doing the unexpected by going for Fargo's legs. Fargo had to leap backward to spare them.

There was no more talk. Julio would not relent until he won, or died. Fargo was always in motion, the toothpick never still. He lost track of where they were. His focus had to be on Julio's knife at all times. Another thrust nearly ripped into his groin. He stabbed at Julio's neck but Julio dodged, skipped, hacked at his midsection.

The fight was taking its toll. Fargo was tiring, just as Julio had predicted. He was a hair slow in lunging to the rear and paid for it with a new rent in his sleeve. Julio smiled, confident. In a knife fight it was not height or weight or sinew that mattered, it was quickness and agility. Julio had those, in excess.

Fargo bumped against a boulder. Flowing to the left, he delivered a blow that would have decapitated Julio if the toothpick were longer—and if it had landed. For Julio was not there when the knife reached him. Fargo crouched, thinking his foe had simply ducked to safety. To his immense surprise, he saw Julio on the ground. The killer had tripped over his own feet.

Julio scrambled upward but he was off balance. He attempted to block a swipe that glanced off his blade and bit into his shoulder. A yelp escaped him. Involuntarily, his arm dropped a few inches.

It was just enough. Fargo did the unexpected now, throwing the toothpick with unerring accuracy. The point imbedded itself near the sternum, at just the right spot. The blade could not miss Julio's heart. Julio stiffened, clutched at his chest, and staggered. He was dead before his body sagged like a wet sack, sprawling facedown.

Fargo sagged himself, abruptly so tired his legs wobbled. He felt an arm slip around him, a warm body support his.

"Are you all right?" Ella asked. "I was getting worried. He was wearing you down. That's why I tripped him."

"You—?" Fargo faced her.

"Don't look at me like that, handsome. I know it was between him and you. I know I had no right to interfere. But I couldn't sit there and let him kill you." Ella smiled sheepishly. "Put me over your knee and paddle me if you want."

Fargo laughed, the tension broken. "I'm not mad—" he began, and had his mouth smothered by hers. Her lips were as delightfully soft as Nina's, her passion as fiery, her body as lush. He would not mind if she kissed him for hours, but she pulled away after only a minute, her eyelids hooded.

"Mmmm. Nice. I might have to do that again sometime."

"I'll look forward to it," Fargo stated. He squinted up at the sun. It wasn't even noon, yet he was tired enough to sleep a week. And his body felt as if a grizzly had used him to sharpen its claws. Walking over to reclaim the toothpick, he said, "Let's collect the horses and the guns and get you back to camp."

"What about you?"

"I've been putting off doing something I should have done the day I rode into Dew Claw." Fargo did not care how weary he was, how badly cut and nicked. Enough was enough. Rowdy Joe Guthrie had sent gunmen to kill him three times. There would not be a fourth.

"You realize that you'll be bucking high odds?"

Fargo certainly did. It was a habit of his he could not seem to break. One day, it might be the death of him.

Maybe this was that day.

8

Early afternoon was Dew Claw's quiet time. Few people were abroad. The Argonauts would not sweep into the mining camp for their nightly spree of gambling, womanizing and hell-raising until much later. Most of those who lived there, doves and gamblers and seedy sorts of every stripe, were not out of bed yet. They were night owls. Sunset, for them, was the same as sunrise for most people. Only the few who conducted business during daylight hours, clerks and business owners and the like, were up and about, and most of them were at their places of business, hard at work.

So it was that hardly anyone saw Skye Fargo enter Dew Claw. He had swung around the camp to come at it from the east, from the opposite direction of Dead Cow Creek. Any lookouts Rowdy Joe Guthrie had posted were likely to be at the west end. At least, that was what Fargo was counting on.

His hand on the Colt, Fargo avoided the main street. Instead, he reined to a side street to the north. Calling it a street was a stretch. It was little more than a narrow aisle between tents pitched so close together a man could not spit without hitting his neighbor's. Snores and low voices droned like the buzz of bees. Occasionally he heard the heated groans of women in the throes of carnal pleasure.

Fargo rose in the stirrups and spied the rear of the Timberline. One of the few real buildings, it stood out like the proverbial sore thumb. There was a door at the back but no windows. Which suited him just fine. He drew rein at the corner and slid down. The stallion knew to stay where it was. He moved to the door, a thin panel of wood that would not withstand a healthy sneeze. The hinges creaked as he pushed.

No outcry greeted him. Fargo stood with his back to the wall until the door was all the way open. Ahead was a storage area crammed with crates and bottles. Beyond that, a long murky hall led toward the front. He glided inside, closing the door behind him so he would not be framed against the rectangle of light.

An Apache could not have been more silent. He passed one door after another, all shut. These were the gaudy parlors where the doves plied their trade from dusk until dawn. At the moment all was still.

Then glass tinkled on glass, and someone laughed. Fargo was almost to the saloon proper. Slowing, he listened to chips clatter, to someone swear good-naturedly. He halted shy of the jamb. Pushing his hat back, he peeked out.

The Timberline was typical. To the left was the bar, a series of wide planks that ran the length of the room. Poker tables dotted the center of the floor. On the right were special tables for faro, roulette, and craps. Besides the bartender, a lanky man busy washing glasses in a basin, only five men were present. Three were at a poker table, old-timers betting pennies on a friendly game of stud.

It was the last two men who piqued Fargo's interest. At a small table near the rear of the bar sat Luke Olinger and the sour-faced gunman, Horner. The latter sullenly nursed a glass of rotgut. Olinger was shuffling a deck over and over again, his limber fingers flipping and whirling individual cards with skillful precision. Fargo started to step into the room, then halted when the front door squeaked.

In came Lester Cavendar. The proprietor of the mercantile was dressed in a suit a full size too small. He acted nervous, his mouth twitching like a rat's whiskers as he glanced right and left as if in fear of being attacked. Squaring his puny shoulders, he marched along the counter to where

Olinger and Horner sat. The gunman gave him a look of undisguised contempt.

Luke Olinger continued to shuffle the deck. He did not glance up, or ask Cavendar to sit. In a tone that implied he thought as highly of the store owner as he did of head lice, he asked, "What is it now, Lester?"

"We need to talk," Cavendar said.

The dandy grinned at Horner. "Now when have I heard that before? What does this make? The twentieth time this month?"

"You ought to put a bell on him, like farmers do with cows," the gunman said. "Tie it around his neck so we'll know he's coming. That way we can lock the door so he can't get in. Keep him from pestering you."

Luke Olinger laughed, then gave Cavendar a hard stare. "See why I keep him around, Lester? He has a sense of humor. Which is more than I can say for you. How many times a day do you crack a smile?"

Lester was peeved and did not hide it. "What does that have to do with anything? I came here to see you on important business and you treat me as if I'm a nuisance! We're in this together. I'll thank you not to forget that."

Olinger placed a hand on the cane that lay next to his right arm, then said so only the businessman and the gunman overheard, "I'll thank *you* to keep your voice down. Our dealings are supposed to be secret. Or have you forgotten?"

Lester's throat bobbed and he gripped the edge of the table. "Now don't get mad. Of course I haven't. But everyone knows we play cards regularly. What's wrong with paying you a friendly visit?"

"We are not friends, Lester. We never have been. We never will be." The dandy sighed. "Simpletons. I am surrounded by simpletons. Is it any wonder things are going the way they are? None of you could beat a ten-year-old at checkers.

"I resent that," Lester declared. "Rowdy Joe is as dumb as they come, I'll grant you. But I happen to have a degree in business management. I happen to have graduated from my class with honors. How can you possibly compare me to him?"

"With honors," Olinger said wearily, as one who had heard the same boast many times before. "Yet here you are, operating a two-bit store in a filthy mining camp in a mud hole in the Rockies. It seems to me that an education isn't all it's claimed to be. Or did you *plan* to start at the bottom and work your way down?"

Cavendar reminded Fargo of a bantam rooster about to fly into a funk. "My store is just a stepping-stone on the road to riches. Both of us stand to leave this Dew Claw with a small fortune if we play our cards right."

Olinger fanned the deck, placed the cards flat on the table, then rippled them back and forth. "What do you know about cards, Lester? What do you know about life, for that matter? I told you not to come here unless it was an emergency. The less we are seen together, the safer we'll be."

"What are you worried about? No one suspects."

"But some might begin to wonder. Soon everyone will hear about Lafferty's claim. Then the others."

"So? They know he liked to gamble. Prospectors do it all the time. In the last week alone I've transferred a couple dozen. It will seem perfectly natural."

"Will it? I hope so. For your sake."

"Is that a threat?"

The gambler stopped rippling the deck. "Threats are for the childish, Lester. I would never waste my breath. When I decide to kill a man, I walk up to him and do it." Olinger sat back. "No, I was referring to that fact that if anyone does become suspicious, the finger of blame will point at you. You're the recorder. You're also the assayer. So you'll be at the top of the lynch mob's list."

A squeamish look came over Cavendar. "Don't talk like that. He's got it all planned out. I trust him. I trust it will work out exactly as he predicted."

"That's another one of the many differences between you

and me, Lester," Olinger said suavely. "You're a weasel, I'm not. You're a miserable miser, I'm not. You don't know how to enjoy life, I do. You're petty and spiteful and shriveled inside like a rotten prune. Yet for all your shortcomings, you trust people. I trust no one, especially him."

"He inspires confidence. Look at how well everything has worked out so far. Rowdy Joe believes in him, too."

"Lester, Rowdy Joe was born with solid bone between his ears. He thinks that all his problems can be solved with his fists or a gun. I would never have become his partner if it were not necessary."

"So long as each of us does his part, I don't see what you have to be concerned about. Rowdy Joe won't do anything without the boss's say-so." Smoothing his coat, Cavendar started to turn. "Talk to you at the next get-together."

"Aren't you forgetting something, Lester?"

"What?"

"Why was it so important you see me?"

Lester put a hand on his cheek. "Damn. I nearly forgot. Murdock was just in my store. Maybe you know him. He's a prospector. His claim is just up the creek from the Young-bloods'." Lester looked to be sure no one else was within earshot. "About noon today, he saw Fargo and Ella Youngblood ride up. Ella was on a fine buttermilk horse, and she was leading a bay with a Mexican rig."

"So Lash and Julio fared no better than Mundy and Rickert," Olinger said thoughtfully. "Joe should have listened to me. I argued against sending them, if you'll recall."

"The boss wanted it done. What else could Joe do?" Cavendar straightened. "I figured you should know right away so you can pass the word along. He'll be as mad as a wet hen. Lash and him were friends."

"Guthrie's not due in Dew Claw until late tonight. Our forty-niner friend and him had important business. They wouldn't tell me what. But I'll make sure they hear about Larson and his partner."

The store owner left. Luke Olinger made a teepee of his slender hands, then shivered.

"What's ailing you?" Horner asked.

"Ever felt as if an ice-cold finger had scraped down your spine?"

"No, can't say as I have. Why?"

"Nothing, Jack. Fetch a bottle, will you? I can use a good, stiff drink."

Fargo did not linger to hear more. Backing up, he hurried to the rear door. A couple of women in form-fitting dresses were sashaying by but they did not give him a second look. Taking the reins, he walked eastward. He had learned a lot, yet nowhere near enough.

Guthrie, Olinger, and one other man were involved in a scheme to get rich. That much Fargo had already known. What he had not known was that Lester Cavendar played an important part. From the sound of things, it was the mystery man who was behind the whole thing. It was the mystery man who told Guthrie and Olinger and Cavendar what to do.

No one had mentioned that Lester was the recorder of claims as well as Dew Claw's official assayer. It was not uncommon, though, for one person to hold both jobs. So long as the person was trustworthy, all went well. When the person wasn't, there was hell to pay.

Fargo came to the back of the huge tent that housed the mercantile. On an impulse he swung between it and the next one and walked to the front hitch rail. After wrapping the reins, he ambled inside, acting as if he did not have a care in the world. An elderly lady and a child were the only customers. A young man in a white apron was stacking merchandise.

"May I help you, sir?"

"I want to see Lester," Fargo said.

"Mr. Cavendar stepped out for a few minutes. He should be back momentarily, if you care to wait."

"Thanks." To occupy himself Fargo browsed through the dry goods. The selection, to Cavendar's credit, was outstanding. There were different varieties of tobacco, cartridges for every make and caliber of rifle and revolver, and a case of sterling knives that included a couple of bowies.

Fargo was examining a pile of thick quilts when into the mercantile bustled its owner. The young clerk said something, and Cavendar turned. His features betrayed surprise. Composing himself, he approached, his hat in hand.

"Mr. Fargo! How nice to see you again. Nina and Mandy were in to get new supplies earlier. I extended them credit, just as I promised you I would."

"Glad to hear it," Fargo said amiably.

"My part-time help, Jerry, tells me that you wanted to see me?"

"Yes." Fargo leaned on the table. "I need information, and I figure you're the one person who can help."

"I'm always ready to do what I can for my fellow man. That business with Nina the other day was just a minor misunderstanding."

Fargo had met blowhards full of hot air before, but Cavendar beat them all. If the man were any more pompous, he would float off like a balloon. "What can you tell me about a prospector by the name of Lafferty?"

Lester's jaw dropped. For several seconds he looked as if he had swallowed a porcupine whole. "What makes you ask?" he inquired in a squeak that would do justice to a mouse.

"I'm checking into something," Fargo hedged. "I figure you must know every last prospector by name since you make a record of all their claims."

"Yes, yes, that I do. Some I know better than others." Lester moved to the knife case and wiped a hand across the top as if checking for dust. "Let me see. Lafferty, was it? That must be Ira Lafferty. The man who first found color on Dead Cow Creek."

"The man whose cow was killed by the mountain lion?"

"None other."

Fargo let Cavendar worry some before saying, "Isn't he one of the prospectors who disappeared?"

Lester scrunched his brow as if thinking. "Yes, I believe you're right. He was the very first. He had come into Dew Claw that day to buy a new pick and shovel. They vanished along with him and his mule."

"So you were one of the last people to see Lafferty alive?"

The question disturbed Lester. He unfolded a quilt, then folded it again. "Now that you mention it, I suppose I was. Although I've heard he stopped for a drink on his way back to his claim. So I wasn't the very last."

"Was it the Timberline he stopped at?"

Cavendar hesitated a bit too long. "I wouldn't really know where." He coughed. "Why all this interest, if I might be so nosy?"

"I was wondering about his claim."

"In what respect? Its ownership? The Argonauts have a rule that a claim must be worked at least once a month or the claimant forfeits all rights. It will be a month, tomorrow, since Lafferty did any digging or panning at his."

"So anyone can file for it? Or will you hold an auction and sell it to the highest bidder, like they do elsewhere?"

Lester turned, all smiles now that he assumed he understood. "So that's what this is about. You want to get your hands on Lafferty's claim." He chuckled. "I admire your initiative. But I'm afraid you're too late."

Fargo waited.

"Ordinarily, I would call a public meeting and sell the site off. But as it so happens, Lafferty signed a sixty-percent interest in his claim over to someone else shortly before he vanished. By law, that party has the right to take over the claim entirely after the thirty-day period." Lester started to walk away.

Fargo was not going to let him off so easily. "Wait a minute. Who did Lafferty sign it over to?"

"That's privileged information."

"Since when? Claims are a matter of public record."

Fargo motioned. "Check for me." The devious schemer dawdled, obviously trying to come up with a valid excuse to refuse. "It's important," Fargo prodded.

"Very well," Lester said, but he dragged his heels all the way down the aisle, stopping several times to rearrange merchandise that did not need arranging. Frowning, he went behind the counter and scanned several shelves. "Hmmm. Now where did I put that entry book?"

Fargo pointed at the top shelf. "Isn't that it there? The one where you wrote 'Claims' on the spine in big black letters?"

"Oh. Mercy. No wonder I wear spectacles." Lester rose onto the tips of his toes. "Here we go." Placing the ledger flat, he opened it and flipped the pages. "I just hope I can find the entry. There are so many, as you can see. Hundreds. It might take me a while."

Rather than punch him in the mouth, Fargo suggested, "Just count back thirty days. That should help."

A snail could have turned the next several pages faster than Lester did. "Ah. Here we go. Ira duly signed a controlling interest in his claim over to Lucas Olinger. It was witnessed by two disinterested parties, Alexander Mundy and Bud Fannin." Lester turned the book so Fargo could read the entry for himself. "See? Everything is perfectly in order."

Disinterested parties? Fannin worked for Olinger, Mundy had been in Rowdy Joe Guthrie's employ. The whole setup reeked to high heaven. But since Fargo did not want Cavendar to suspect exactly how much he knew, he innocently asked, "Why would Lafferty do such a thing?"

"I'm the recorder. I make entries. I don't snoop into the personal affairs of those who require my services." Lester crossed his arms. "But, between you and me, I believe Ira got in over his head at a card game. His penchant for gambling was well known. He didn't have enough money to cover his losses, so he signed over the partial interest in his claim as collateral until he could pay the debt off. As simple as that. And, again, perfectly legal."

Fargo's mind raced. Had all the men who disappeared

done the same thing? "What about Brian Youngblood? Did he sign his claim over to anyone?"

"I can answer that without even looking. No, he did not."

So much for that idea, Fargo mused. He wished that he knew the names of the other prospectors who had vanished. But then again. Lester would go running to Olinger if he nosed around too much. So maybe it was best he not pry any further for the time being. "I'm obliged for your help," he said, making for the flap.

"Think nothing of it," Cavendar said happily, with a cheery wave.

Fargo had a lot to ponder. He waited until he was clear of Dew Claw and traveling to the west. When he was convinced no one trailed him, he reviewed everything he had learned. There had to be a pattern. There had to be something the missing men had in common. Something Guthrie and Olinger wanted to get their hands on. The gold claims were the logical prize. But Youngblood had not signed his over. Why had he been murdered, then? Had he stumbled onto their secret?

At least now Fargo understood why Luke Olinger was worried. Since the thirty days were almost up, others would inquire about the status of Lafferty's claim. The news would spread like wildfire. Some would rightfully suspect that Olinger had a hand in Lafferty's disappearance. Maybe Lafferty's friends would cause trouble.

Important questions remained unanswered. Who was the mystery man behind the operation? What part did Rowdy Joe Guthrie play? How were Guthrie and Olinger linked? And what was Lester Cavendar's involvement?

Fargo had learned one tidbit of importance. Rowdy Joe was expected in the mining camp sometime late that night. He would pay Guthrie a visit. The man had a lot to answer for, and Fargo intended to see that he did.

Eventually Fargo cut to the main trail. Gold hounds eager to get to Dew Claw early and lose their day's earnings passed him with smiles and waves. A few pointed and whispered.

His clash with Mundy had earned him a reputation he did not particularly want. A new trend was taking place in the West, a trend Fargo was not fond of. It was most prevalent down in Texas, and in towns and communities all along the U.S.–Mexican border. But it was spreading.

It had to do with those who lived and died by the gun, with the badmen and assassins. With hardcases who had no scruples about blowing holes in anyone who crossed them. Shootists, some called them. Out-and-out killers was more like it. Yet many people treated them as if they were special.

It had gotten so that those who earned the most notches on their pistols were held in the highest esteem. Toughs and bullies and young hotheads wanting to add to their reputations went around looking for trouble just to add another notch.

Fargo wanted no part of it. It was bad enough he was widely known for his exploits as a scout and a marksman. He did not want to be added to the growing ranks of notorious gunmen.

The change was just one of many taking place. Fargo was a young man, but he knew how it had been in the old days. He had many close friends, mountain men and trappers and voyageurs, who shared tales of how the West once was, and how different it had become.

Once, the Rockies had been home to a paltry handful of whites. Now white men swarmed over the mountains like hungry locusts in their lust to unearth gold and silver. Once, the prairie had been home to Indians and wildlife. Now farms and ranches were springing up in ever-growing numbers. Once, a man could count the settlements between the Mississippi River and the Pacific Ocean on two hands. Now there were so many a man had to tally them on sheets of paper.

Fargo loved the wilderness. He loved to explore uncharted territory, the wild tracts where few whites, if any, had ever gone. Plenty remained, but each year the influx shrank their number and size.

A friend of his, an oldster who had seen more sunsets than there were whiskers on Fargo's chin, claimed that one day the wilderness would be gone. That there would come a time when cities and towns would cover the land from shining sea to shining sea. His friend even believed most of the buffalo would be killed off, just as the beaver had nearly been wiped out a few decades ago.

Fargo had scoffed at the silly notion. Then he got to thinking. To recollecting how civilization had spread from the Atlantic to the Mississippi in a span of five generations. He had to wonder what changes the next hundred years would bring. Would the last of the wild places be tamed by the plow and the pitchfork? Would all the Indians be forced off their lands, as had been done back East? Would the bear and the buffalo and the eagle be slaughtered to the point where only a few survived?

It was a sobering notion.

The claims along Dead Cow Creek came into view. Fargo brought the Ovaro to a trot, anxious to partake of the special supper Ella had promised. Suddenly he realized all was not as it should be. Between where he was and a bend several hundred feet away were over twenty tents and rickety shacks. Yet there wasn't a single soul in sight.

A racket rose from around the bend. It did not prepare him for what he saw. Prospectors were scurrying along both banks, poking into every gully, every nook, every thicket. Some were mounted, some were not. They were searching for someone, or something. That much was clear. Fargo figured another Argonaut had disappeared. Or maybe there was a simpler explanation. Maybe a mountain lion or a bear had attacked someone and the beast was being hunted.

Shouts rolled back and forth.

"She's not up this wash!"

"What about the gorge?"

"Stan and his boys are checkin'."

"Anyone combed those scrub trees south of here?"

"Remember, she's wearing brown pants and a green shirt?"

She? Fargo galloped on down Dead Cow, scattering searchers right and left. A motley crowd had gathered at the Youngblood claim. Ella was there, with Barclay and Fiddlemeyer and some of the other leaders. All wore long faces.

Ella saw him and ran to meet him halfway, crying out before he came to stop, "Skye! Thank God! She's gone! They snatched her!"

"Nina," Fargo said, mad he had not been on hand to prevent it.

"No. Not Nina." Ella's terror drained the blood from her face. "Mandy! Someone stole my little sister!"

9

Ella Youngblood did something she had sworn she would never do. She broke down in front of dozens of strangers. The moment Fargo dismounted, she threw herself into his arms and sobbed in great racking heaves. Fargo held her close, feeling the warmth of her body, the dampness of her tears as they flowed from her chin onto his neck. He did not try to stop her. She needed to get it out.

Fully five minutes went by before Ella straightened, sniffled, and wiped her nose with her sleeve. Her eyes were red, her cheeks slick. "I'm awful sorry," she apologized. "I didn't mean to do that."

"I'd do the same if I were in your shoes," Fargo said. The feeblest of grateful smiles curled her lovely lips. He surveyed the throng again. "Where's Nina?"

"Off helping in the search. We figured one of us should stay here in case Mandy is found."

"How did it happen? Tell me everything."

Ella nodded. But when she started to speak, more tears flowed. Harvey materialized and held out a crumpled bandanna. Fargo accepted it, gave it to Ella. Bravely trying not to cry, she dabbed her face, the bandanna leaving streaks of dirt in its wake. No one laughed. No one even grinned. Harvey looked horrified, and thrusting his hands into his pockets, he pulled out another, cleaner bandanna, which he shoved at Ella, taking the dirty one back. Sheepishly, he slunk off like a puppy that had just piddled indoors.

Fargo waited. As worried as he was about sweet little

Mandy, enough people were scouring the brush for her at the moment that one more would not make much of a difference. There had to be over a hundred, with more arriving from upstream every few minutes as word was carried from claim to claim. Barclay was directing the search effort, sending teams to new areas that needed to be searched.

Art Jessup hurried up, his pudgy face caked with sweat. "Sorry to bother you, Ella," he said, "but Nina sent me. We've gone over every square foot of the spot where she was last seen. All we found was this." From behind his back he brought out a doll. It had seen a lot of use. The dress was soiled, the hair stringy, and one foot was missing. "It was lying near the creek."

"Oh God!" Ella said, and clasped it to her as if it were Mandy herself. "Miss Maple! Mandy has had this since she was four. She would never let anything happen to it." More sobs escaped her. "Who would want to hurt a little girl? What kind of brute would do such a thing?"

Art had no answer.

"What about Felix?" Ella asked.

"No sign of the dog, either. Sorry." Jessup went over to join Fiddlemeyer and Barclay.

Ella sagged against Fargo, her forehead on his chest. "I can't take this, Skye. I don't know what I'll do if they can't find her. It's all my fault. I should have been paying more attention. I shouldn't have let her run off like I did." She looked at him and repeated the question she had asked Art Jessup. "What kind of vile brute would do such a thing?"

Fargo did not reply. What could he say that would not upset her even more? Only the worst sort of scum would hurt a child. It was practically unheard of. Especially on the frontier, where harming children wreaked swift and terrible retribution. The luxury of a trial was dispensed with. Guilty parties were marched to the nearest tree and given a hemp necktie.

Even the worst of cutthroats would not think to kill a kid. Doing so crossed an invisible line no man could ever re-cross. He was branded with the dark stain for the rest of his life. It was the final perversion, the act of the totally depraved.

"Feel up to telling me what happened?" Fargo asked.

Ella nodded, but it was several minutes before she stopped weeping and sniffling. "I was at the sluice. Nina was in the tent, sewing her dress. Mandy was playing with Miss Maple." She stopped, pressed the doll to her bosom, and softly groaned.

"Take your time. If you'd rather not talk about it right now, I'll understand."

"No, no, I don't mind." Ella shook herself and went on. "The dog started barking and ran off up Dead Cow Creek. Sometimes Felix does that. He can be such a bother. I told Mandy to fetch him so he wouldn't pester anyone."

If it were Fargo, he would keep the mongrel tied to a rope. But people were funny where their pets were concerned. They'd let a cat or dog tear up their furniture, pee on their carpet, chew their most prized possession, and still claim it was the most adorable animal that ever lived.

Ella took a breath. "I didn't think much of it. Mandy skipped off to get him and I went on working. When I did look up, she was going around the bend to the west, yelling for Felix to come back. I figured she would return in a few minutes, like she's always done."

"But she didn't," Fargo coaxed after Ella was quiet for a while.

"No. I thought the dog must be giving her a hard time. So I went to find them. I walked and walked but never saw either."

"Did you stop to ask if anyone else had?"

"Finally I did, yes. No one recollected doing so, so I backtracked. Bill Wessman, who has a claim near where Poverty Creek flows into Dead Cow, told me he'd seen Felix go running up Poverty Creek earlier, with Mandy close behind."

Fargo had learned enough. "How far is this other creek?" He wanted to help out.

"About a quarter of a mile to the west. It's the first tributary you come to. No one has ever found any gold along it, so—" Ella grabbed him by the arm when he turned toward the Ovaro "Wait. There's more, Skye. God help me, there's more."

"You saw who took her?"

"No, no. I wish to hell I had. But—" Ella sagged, tears flowing freely. Fargo held her, stroking her hair, and she seemed to gather strength from the contact. "Bill said that just before Felix went by a big man on horseback had ridden into Poverty Creek. Bill thought that Felix was following him."

Fargo's pulse quickened. A big man? Could it be the same one he had chased the other night? "Did Wessman say what this man looked like?"

"Bill wasn't paying much attention until Felix went by, barking his fool head off. That's when he stopped panning. He hollered to Mandy to ask her what was going on but she hurried on up Poverty Creek, too, without answering."

"He didn't go after her?"

Ella shook her head. "He's all torn up about it, but we can't really blame him. Mandy and the dog were always running somewhere or other. He figured the rider must be someone she knew. It never occurred to him that anyone would want to hurt her. Why should it? Who in their right mind would harm a child?"

No one. Fargo stepped into the stirrups. "I'm going to Poverty Creek."

Ella grasped his leg. "Find her. Please, Skye. She's so sweet. So innocent. I'd die if anything happened to her."

Fargo was not one to let his emotions get the better of him, but fiery fury welled up as he galloped westward. This had to be more of Guthrie's doing, probably at the bidding of the mystery man who was behind the scheme. What purpose it served was anyone's guess. Maybe it was their way of getting back at the sisters for daring to help him.

Men scoured both banks. Long lines roamed adjacent

hills. Mounted searchers roved at will, even into dense thickets that tore at rider and mount alike.

Poverty Creek was a mere ribbon of water, barely deep enough to drown a fly. Argonauts were going up and down all the gullies and ravines it bisected. Fargo saw a slender figure barking instructions.

Nina pivoted as he reined up. "Skye!" She flew to him, embracing him before he had both feet on the ground. Trembling like a leaf, she whispered, "I reckon you've heard. I'm so scared. So afraid something awful has happened."

"Has anyone found tracks?"

"Yes," Nina drew back. "None of Mandy's, though. Only Felix and the rider he was after."

"Show me." Fargo was not going to waste another minute. She clasped his hand and hastened to a strip of bare earth that bordered the creek. "Here's some."

The ground was soft, the impressions as clear as those of a cookie cutter in fresh dough. The tracks of the horse were deepest, which was only natural given its weight. It had gone by at a trot, as the spacing of its hooves demonstrated. Felix's paw prints showed that he had been barreling along like a bat out of hell trying to overtake it. Then there were a few of Mandy's footprints. She had been running, too.

Further on the soil became rock-hard. The prints of the horse were the only ones that showed, and even they were incomplete. A scrape here, a gouge there, chips of missing rock, they all told Fargo the rider had gone another fifty yards, then suddenly halted. He had to look and look before he found a partial paw mark that proved Felix had at last caught up. What happened after that was a mystery because the tracks gave no clue.

"Would Felix have attacked him?" Fargo wondered aloud. That there was no blood was encouraging. Apparently, the rider hadn't shot the mongrel dead right on the spot. He could not find a trace of Mandy's tracks, which did not mean much. She was so small and light they would not show up.

"He's snapped at people but he's never attacked anyone," Nina said. "Except Indians once," she said, amending her statement. "And a drunk in St. Louis."

"Why did he chase this man so far? Does he go after riders sometimes?" Fargo knew of dogs that would chase anything that moved. Many a time he had ridden past homesteads and whatnot and had miserable curs yap at the Ovaro's hooves.

Nina was as distraught as her sister but she held back her tears. Wrapping her arms around her chest, she said sorrowfully, "Yes, I'm sorry to say. He goes after horses and mules on occasion. We always punish him, and I thought we had cured him of the habit. Guess I was wrong."

There was no way of telling how long the rider had stood there. Probably not long. Fargo hiked further, bent low. The horse tracks bore due south. Damned if Felix's prints weren't right next to them, the horse and dog trotting merrily along side-by-side, like they were the best of friends. Which meant that Mandy must be *on* the horse, riding double. Either that, or she had been thrown over the saddle against her will. "Would Felix protect Mandy if someone tried to hurt her?"

"Would he ever! He was too protective at times. He even snapped at Pa once or twice when Pa scolded her for misbehaving. That drunk I mentioned nearly lost his arm when he put a hand on Mandy's shoulder and she got spooked and screamed."

Fargo turned to the Ovaro. "I won't be back until I find her. Tell Ella."

"Let me get my horse and tag along."

"I work faster alone." Fargo forked leather, touched his hat brim, and lightly applied his spurs. Nina made no attempt to hide her disappointment, but it was best this way. It went without saying that every minute of delay could prove costly.

Fargo had to admit he did not know what to make of Mandy's abduction. She would not have gone off willingly with a stranger. Yet there was no sign Felix had tried to prevent the man from taking her. Did that mean she knew the rider, then? Could it have been Rowdy Joe Guthrie? The idea was not as far-fetched as it seemed. She and Guthrie were well acquainted; Rowdy Joe had paid her to watch "his" hitch rail in Dew Claw. So it was entirely possible Guthrie had lured her off. But why? What did he hope to gain? Surely even Guthrie would not be stupid enough to harm a child?

The only way to answer all his questions was to find them. Fargo followed the meager sign southward for a while. Then the tracks bore to the southeast.

Whoever the man was, he was not very skilled at shaking pursuit. He stuck to fairly rocky ground but still crossed tracts of bare earth now and then, tracts where his mount's hoofprints were as plain as day. He did not try to erase the tracks. He made no attempt to double back. Nor did he wind through nearby densely wooded sections, as any seasoned outlaw would have done to slow down those after him. The kidnapper's sole concern appeared to be to spirit the girl away quickly.

Perhaps with good cause. Some prospectors had tried to track him but lost the sign about a mile from Poverty Creek. Fargo overtook them as they were crisscrossing a gulch. Someone he knew was in charge of things.

"Howdy, Fargo," Barney Fiddlemeyer said. "We sure do keep runnin' into one another, don't we? It's darned awful about the girl. Must make you wish you'd listened to us the other night and taken us up on our request to have Rowdy Joe Guthrie killed."

"Have your men pull back, Fiddlemeyer."

"How's that?"

"I don't want them to wipe out the trail. It happened once before, when Brian Youngblood was killed."

Fiddlemeyer resented being treated as if he were incompetent. "I wasn't even there then. Nor were half of these boys. Trust me. We know what we're doing. We'll pick up the son of a bitch's tracks again soon enough."

"Just have them pull back," Fargo said.

"Now see here," Fiddlemeyer responded. "Who are you to tell us what to do? The more of us searching, the sooner we'll find her. Right?"

"Not necessarily." Fargo had no inclination to debate the issue. Putting his hand on the Colt, he said, "I won't say it a third time."

"You have your gall, mister. But you don't scare me none. You won't kill a man who's not trying to kill you."

The Colt was out and level in a heartbeat. "True," Fargo admitted. "But I sure as hell wouldn't mind shooting your ear off. Or maybe a couple of toes."

"What nonsense. You're bluffing. We're both on the same side."

The boom of the revolver was exceptionally loud thanks to the high gully walls. The slug whistled past Fiddlemeyer's left ear. His mare pranced and whinnied, and he had to fight to get her under control. The other Argonauts stopped and stared, unsure of what was going on.

"Are you loco?" Fiddlemeyer fumed, as mad as a wet cat.

"No. I'm in a hurry. And I don't want you interfering. Now do as I told you. Next time I won't miss."

After swearing a blue streak, Fiddlemeyer called to his fellow gold seekers. They did not like being made to leave. A few looked as if they were angry enough to tear into Fargo with their bare hands. He ignored them and rode down the middle of the gully to the far end where solid rock extended for a considerable distance. No wonder they had lost the sign. By pure luck the kidnapper had stumbled on a godsend.

Or was it luck? Maybe Fargo was not giving the man enough credit. Maybe the kidnapper had been making for this particular spot all along.

Faint scratches and scrapes sufficed to steer Fargo in a new direction, to the north. The rider had held to a gallop. At length the direction changed again. This time to the north-east. Fargo was so intent on the prints that he did not think to look behind him for quite a while. When he did, he was mildly surprised to see Fiddlemeyer and company several hundred yards back. Reining up, he mulled over what to do, then rose in the stirrups to beckon them.

Fiddlemeyer was not quite sure of the reception they would get. When they were still a dozen yards out he said loudly, "Don't get all hot under the collar! We haven't ham-pered you one bit. I just figured you might need us in case the jasper who took the girl has friends."

Fargo was thinking the same thing. If Rowdy Joe was to blame, sooner or later Guthrie would rejoin his gang. Alone, he would be outgunned. "So long as you stay behind me, you're welcome to tag along."

"Fickle feller, ain't you?" Fiddlemeyer said. He jabbed a thumb at the ground. "But you sure as hell can track. We'd never have gotten this far on our own. Half the time I'd have sworn you were traveling blind, then there would be a print that even we couldn't miss. How do you do it, Fargo?" Sud-denly Fiddlemeyer blinked and smacked a cheek in aston-ishment. "Fargo! Skye Fargo? Damn! Why didn't it hit me sooner? Everyone has heard of you. Ain't you the one they call the Trailsman?"

Fargo nodded.

The nine Argonauts were also impressed. "My God!" one of them exclaimed. "This is like meetin' Daniel Boone or Kit Carson! I heard about that shootin' match you were in over to Springfield, Missouri. Where you were up against Dottie Wheatridge and Vin Chadwell."

"And I heard about that shoot-out you had down Durango way," another man chimed in. "The newspaper said you killed that famous bandit, El Gato, with your bare hands."

There were days when Fargo wished he could take every self-serving journalist and every writer of dreadful penny novels and dump them all in quicksand. Many warped the truth on purpose to boost sales, turning ordinary events into sensational stories, with no regard for how their lies affected the lives of those they wrote about. "No, the Utes killed El Gato. I can't claim credit."

"Skye Fargo," Fiddlemeyer said again, in awe. "I bet Rowdy Joe doesn't know who you are, either, or he'd never have stomped on you like he done."

"Not and let you live," commented someone else.

Fargo sighed and rode on. Being well known had its drawbacks. Which was why he did not go around advertising who he was, like Joe Meek and Mike Fink and others had been prone to do. Fink was forever fighting would-be toughs, while Meek had gotten to the point where he never knew when someone might stick a blade into his back just to shut him up.

More tracks appeared as the terrain changed. It soon was apparent that if they kept on as they were doing, they would come to the trail linking Dead Cow Creek to Dew Claw. Fargo half expected the kidnapper had gone to the mining camp but the prints crossed the trail and forged on to the north.

"Where does this polecat think he's heading?" Fiddlemeyer remarked. "There's nothin' yonder but mountains full of Injuns and silvertips."

"No fit place for a child, that's for certain sure," said a short prospector.

Time became more of a factor than ever. The sun was on its downward arc. In a couple of hours they would lose the light. Fargo picked up the pace. Mandy was not going to spend one night alone with her abductor if he could help it.

"Hey! Lookee there!" a prospector hollered. "On that ridge!"

Fargo had already spotted the glimmer. Sunlight being reflected off metal or some other shiny surface. Guthrie might have a spyglass. If so, Rowdy Joe knew they were hard on his heels. Less than half an hour behind, if that.

"I can't wait to get my hands on the varmint," Fiddlemeyer declared. "We'll escort him to the nearest tree and have him do a strangulation jig."

"Not until I find out a few things," Fargo said.

"Like what? Why he took the sprout?"

"That will do for a start."

Even the gold hounds could read the sign now. The rider had gone up a barren slope, his horse kicking loose enough dirt and small stones to start a small avalanche. It was almost as if he had done it deliberately.

Fargo would not put it past the man to lie in ambush and pick them off as they came over the crest, so he lowered his hand to the Colt when the Ovaro reached the top. He was not going to be taken by surprise. What awaited him, though, came as a total shock.

On a small boulder sat a petite figure. Her short legs dangling, she beamed cheerfully. Nearby lay Felix, his head resting on his forepaws. He rose and moved in front of the boulder as they drew closer.

"Skye! I'm so glad it's you who came!" Mandy said.

Fargo scanned the ridge. Not enough vegetation grew to hide a cat. Her kidnapper was gone. Swirls of dust at the opposite end verified it. He came to a stop and climbed down. Felix bared his fangs but at a word from the girl quieted and moved aside. "Are you all right?" Fargo asked, picking her up.

"Of course. Why wouldn't I be?" Mandy responded. She hugged him. "Now we can go have some of that pie Ella promised to bake us."

Fiddlemeyer and the prospectors were just as confused by the turn of events. They whispered to one another, Lester scratching his beard as if he had fleas. "What in tarnation are you doing here, girlie?"

"Waiting for Skye and you, Mr. Fiddlemeyer," Mandy said.

"You knew we were following you?"

"Sure. He told me. He saw you through his telescope.

He's had it since before I was born. I looked, and I could see you a long ways off."

"Who?" Barney asked. "Who was it snatched you? Tell us the coyote's name so we can string him up when we find him."

Mandy balled her fists. "He said you would want to do that, but you'll do no such thing! It wouldn't be nice!"

"Nice?" Fiddlemeyer declared. "Girl, he stole you. Took you right out from under your sister's nose. There's no telling what he would have done if we hadn't caught up with him so quicklike. And that's wrong. It's pure evil. He's bad, bad to the marrow."

"He is not!" Mandy was incensed. "He's the nicest man who ever lived! I won't let you talk about him like that! Hear me? I won't!"

Fargo sought to soothe her. "Calm down, little one. We were worried about you, is all. Your sisters, too. They were so upset they were crying."

"Gosh. Really?" Mandy said. "We'd better get back then, so I can tell them they had nothing to fret about. He'd never hurt me. Not in a million years."

Fiddlemeyer frowned and motioned. "You don't know that, girl. Now tell us who it was. We'll spread the word and have him decorating a cottonwood before the week is out. Just see if we don't."

Mandy's lower lip commenced to quiver. Fargo glared at Barney but the lunkhead did not know when to shut up.

"Out with it, child! We've come a long way. We've eaten a lot of dust and we're sore and tired. So unless you want a spanking you'll never forget, be smart and fess up to who it was."

"No one is going to spank me," Mandy declared, sounding frightened.

"We'll see about that," Barney huffed.

"No one is going to spank her," Fargo echoed. Maybe Nina was right about the old coot. Fargo had never met anyone so all-fired eager to mete out spankings—to females of all ages. It left him with a problem. He'd thought that Fiddlemeyer could take Mandy back while he went on after the kidnapper before the man got too much of a head start. But it would hardly be right to leave her in the care of someone she must be scared to death of. Someone who would tan her backside given any little excuse.

"Spare the rod and spoil the child," Barney quoted his favorite line. "No wonder kids today grow up doomed to perdition."

Fargo had an inspiration. He couldn't go after the kidnapper, but that didn't mean the man had to get clean away. "Why don't you and the others go on? Try and catch the gent we're after before it gets dark."

"Where will you be?"

"Taking Mandy to her sisters. I'll rejoin you as soon as I can."

The child squirmed and cried, "No! No! Let him be!"

Fiddlemeyer smirked and wheeled his mount. "You heard the Trailsman, boys! Let's light a shuck! By nightfall there will be some human fruit swinging in these parts." Grinning at the prospect, he headed a rush toward the edge of the ridge.

Amanda Youngblood twisted violently, seeking to be released. "Stop them! Please, Skye! They have no call to hurt him! He didn't do anything wrong."

"He stole you." Fargo set her down but held her by the shoulders so she could not run off. "Who is he, Mandy? I promise not to tell anyone if you'll confide in me. Even Ella and Nina. But I need to know."

She looked at him and opened her mouth as if to reveal her secret. Then she uttered a choking sob. It was harbinger to a torrent of tears. Face buried in her hands, she wailed over and over again, "I can't! I just can't!"

Fargo stared after the departing prospectors, wondering. Just wondering.

10

The yelling went on for over half an hour. Before that there had been almost an hour of pleading spiced by threats of a spanking. And prior to *that* an hour of sugary sweet persuasion no more effective than any of the rest. The outcome was that Ella Youngblood stormed from the tent and came over to the fire, muttering under her breath. She caught Skye Fargo staring at her and gave voice to her anger. "Did you hear all that? The ornery brat! Nothing worked! She won't tell us no matter what we do!" Ella kicked at the ground, scattering dirt on the flames. They sputtered but did not go out. "I don't understand! Neither does Nina. We just don't know what has gotten into her."

"Give her time," Fargo said. "Maybe she'll come around."

"And cows will sprout wings and fly," Ella responded. "Mandy has always been a stubborn little cuss, but never *this* stubborn. Why won't she tell us who stole her? Who is she trying to protect?"

Fargo did not offer an opinion.

"Rowdy Joe, maybe?" Ella speculated. "But why? What's he ever done for her?" She smacked her hands together and glared at the world. "I wish to hell you had caught the son of bitch so we'd know who it was."

So did Fargo. He had brought Mandy back, then ridden like a madman to catch up with Fiddlemeyer's boys. Shortly before sunset, he did, only to learn they had lost the trail again. He backtracked but the sun relinquished the heavens to the stars before he could find where they had gone astray. Since he had not deemed it wise to have the sisters spend the night alone, he'd returned to Dead Cow Creek. Fiddlemeyer and the others had gone to their claims. And here he had sat, sipping coffee, while Nina and Ella tried their best to get their younger sister to reveal the identity of her abductor.

"If anything had happened to her—" Ella said, but did not finish. It was a warm night yet she shuddered as if cold. "Losing Ma and Pa was bad enough. I couldn't take it if I lost one of my sisters, too."

The slow clomp of hooves alerted Fargo to an approaching horseman. More likely than not it was an Argonaut. They were always coming and going. But Fargo lowered his hand to his Colt anyway.

Ella stared morosely into the fire. "Nina and I will take turns watching over Mandy. We're not leaving her by herself. Whoever tried to steal her might try again."

Fargo agreed it was a good idea.

"Harve Barclay wanted to post men at our claim but I told him no. I don't want to impose on anyone." Ella hardened. "Besides, we can take care of ourselves."

The horseman was an indistinct outline in the night, growing more distinct with every stride. Fargo noticed that the man's hat was shaped like the rounded bottom of a bowl, and he rose. None of the prospectors wore bowlers. The gleam of firelight off spectacles let him know who it was. "You've got company," he announced.

Ella turned as Lester Cavendar reined up. He sat a saddle about as well as a lump of coal, and dismounted with all the grace of a wingless duck. "Evening, Miss Youngblood," he said, smoothing his jacket. "Nice night, isn't it?"

"What kind of stupid question is that?" Ella tore into him. "Haven't you heard what happened, Lester?"

"Yes, yes, I have," Cavendar replied, his thin lips forming into a pasty smile. "And you have my heartfelt sympathy for the ordeal you've been through." He glanced at the tent. "I trust the child is all right? Or so I've heard."

"Mandy is fine," Ella said. She squinted at the merchant as if he were a strange bug that had just crawled out from under a rock. "Pardon my manners, but exactly what in the hell are you doing here? You've never set foot on Dead Cow Creek before that I know of."

"No, I haven't," Lester admitted, smoothing his jacket again even though it did not need it. "But these are special circumstances. I came because of our friendship."

Ella looked at Fargo. "Did I hear him right? He just called us friends? This from the skinflint who wouldn't extend us any more credit unless we paid our bill in full?"

Lester coughed. "Now, now. What's done is done. Water over the dam. But I've always thought of you as a friend, Ella. Why else did I make that offer to you?"

Ella addressed Fargo again. "Some offer! When we first went in to talk to him about our credit, he said he would buy our claim from us instead. Went on and on about how this is no life for ladies. How we should go back to the States. Live with our aunt and uncle in Ohio."

"And I still maintain that is best for all three of you," Lester declared. "Look at today. You came close to losing Amanda. Is that what you want? Is the gold worth her life?" He stood straighter. "I say it isn't. And I came out here to give you a chance to quit this horrid life. I'm still prepared to buy your claim. You can leave tomorrow. In a month you'll be with your aunt, safe and sound. You can start over again living normal lives."

"How kind of you," Ella said bitterly.

"You're being unfair," Lester protested. "As I recall, you never even let me tell you how much I'm prepared to offer. I assure you, it is quite generous." He paused. "How does ten thousand dollars sound?"

Ella gawked.

"That's right, my dear," Lester said smugly. "You heard me. Ten thousand dollars. Five times as much as any claim along this creek is worth. More than many people earn in a lifetime. More than enough for you and your sisters to get by."

"I don't know what to say," Ella responded.

"Say yes," Lester goaded. "You can pick up the money on your way through Dew Claw. And to further demonstrate how wrongly you've misjudged me, I'll throw in enough supplies to last you the whole trip."

"Ten thousand!" Ella was dazzled by the sum. "You have that much cash on hand, Lester? Or would it be a draft on a bank?"

Cavendar thought she had swallowed the bait. His grin was like that of a weasel that had a rabbit cornered. "Better than either of those, my dear. I'm prepared to give you the ten thousand in gold. Nuggets and dust, mostly."

"Where did you get a small fortune like that?"

"What does it matter, my dear?" Lester asked. "Surely you're not going to look a gift horse in the mouth? Accept, and by this time tomorrow your cares and woes will be over. Just think of how much benefit it will be. All the things you can do. All the dreams you can make real."

Ella put a hand to her head. "I just don't know. It sounds too good to be true. I need time to think."

"What is there to think about?" Lester kept the pressure on. "You'll never have to fret about Mandy having enough to eat or there being clothes on her back ever again. That alone is sufficient."

Fargo squatted and took a swallow of coffee. It tasted bitter going down. He made no comment. Whatever the sisters decided would be fine by him.

"Yes, it is," Ella answered. "But Nina and I still need to talk it over. And right now she's tucking Mandy in. So how about if we ride in to see you in the morning? We'll have made up our minds by then."

Lester fidgeted. "I'd much rather you agreed now. But if you can't, you can't. In the morning will have to do." He finally chose to acknowledge Fargo's presence. "And what about you, mister? Where will you go once they're gone?"

"Who says I'm leaving?" Fargo rejoined.

"Well, I just assumed you wouldn't stick around," Lester said. "You're their friend, aren't you? I imagined you would want to escort them back to the States. If word leaks out about all the gold they'll be carrying, every cutthroat within a hundred miles will be after them."

"I'm not going anywhere until my business here is done."

Lester tried not to show how upset he was, and failed. "What business is that, if I might inquire?"

"I want to get my hands on the man who took Mandy." Fargo did not care to let slip exactly how much he knew, so he added, "I'm also after those who are behind the disappearances. Everyone involved deserves to be strung up."

"You're going to go after them all by yourself? You're just one man. They have a whole gang. What chance would you have?"

Even Ella caught the mistake Cavendar had made. "Hold on, Lester. None of us have any idea how many are involved. Unless you know something I don't?"

The conspirator's nervous laugh was like the braying of a donkey. "Not at all, Miss Youngblood. I merely took it for granted there must be more than one. It flies in the face of logic that a lone killer is to blame."

Fargo liked to see Cavendar squirm like the worm he was. "It doesn't matter how many are involved. It's the leaders I'm after. Kill them and the rest of the gang will fall apart."

"Kill them? With no trial? No due process? No chance for them to defend themselves in a court of law?"

"Was Ira Lafferty given a chance to defend himself? Or any of the other men who vanished? No. They were murdered, and their bodies were buried where no one will ever find them. What due process did they get?"

Lester's smirk almost earned him a punch in the mouth. "We can't be positive the missing men are dead. Maybe they simply got tired of breaking their backs for a pittance and rode out."

"Without telling anyone?" Fargo envisioned wringing

Cavendar's scrawny neck, and smiled. "Hardly. No one will ever see them again, and you damn well know it. Those who are to blame must pay."

"It sounds to me as if you've appointed yourself judge, jury, and executioner," Lester persisted. "Does anyone have that right?"

"Ask the six prospectors who were murdered."

"You mean seven, Skye," Ella corrected him. "Seven men have gone missing, all told, counting my pa."

"That's right," Fargo said. "How could I have forgotten?" He had not taken his eyes off Lester. "All those men. Killed so someone can steal their claims right out from under them. Steal them legally so no one can raise a fuss."

Ella glanced at him. "Hold on. What are you talking about? What do *you* know that I don't?"

Fargo rose. "I know it's time for Lester to leave." He had said too much but maybe it was for the best. In poker, sometimes the only way to get someone to show their hand was to call their bluff. "He has an important meeting to get to later on. One he better not miss."

"What meeting?" Ella asked, confused. "Lester, what's going on between the two of you? I'd like to be filled in."

"Ask your friend," Cavendar said gruffly. He had enough backbone to remark, "Advise him he had better sleep with one eye open. Sticking his nose where it doesn't belong could prove fatal. The men who killed those gold hounds won't hesitate to hunt down and kill anyone who stands in their way."

"You have it backwards," Fargo said.

"How so?"

"I'm the one hunting *them*."

Lester nodded once at Ella, then spun and scrambled back onto the tall bay. "Remember my offer, dear woman. I'll open my store early so you can get your gold that much sooner. Be seeing you." Doffing the bowler, he reined around and was gone.

Ella took a few steps as if she were going to call out to

him, then she rotated and said in bewilderment, "I didn't understand any of that. Why do you dislike him so much? Sure, he's a miser and has the personality of a goat, but otherwise he's not so bad."

Fargo stretched. The candle in the tent had gone out. "Nina and Mandy have turned in. You should do the same. I'll stand guard."

"You're not going to tell me, are you?"

"I have to leave in a few hours," Fargo mentioned. "You should get some rest while you can. I'll wake you when I go."

"Go where?" Ella came around the fire and grabbed him by the arm. "Quit being so damn mysterious! I have a right to know, don't I? It's my sister who was stolen. And my father forfeited his life."

Fargo raised a hand to her chin and gently traced its profile with a fingertip. He would love to confide what he suspected. But it would break her heart. And what if he was wrong? "Until I have more proof I'd rather not say anything."

Ella stamped a foot. "You're just like every other man! Pigheaded and tight-lipped. I thought you would be more considerate than most."

"Nice try." Fargo chuckled. "Now go turn in."

For over a minute Ella didn't move or speak. Then she stretched, as he had just done, closing her eyes and tilting her lovely features to the fire, her bosom swelling against her shirt. The alluring image she presented was enough to set any man's groin to stirring. "I'm not at all tired," she said. "I couldn't sleep if I tried."

Fargo bent to the coffeepot. "Want me to pour you a cup, then?"

"No, thank you." Ella clasped her hands behind her back and stared off across Dead Cow Creek. "I'd rather go for a walk. Care to come along?"

"What about your sisters?"

"Oh, we won't go very far," Ella assured him. She pointed

at a knoll on the other side. "Just there. It's a great place to sit and admire the stars. And we can see everything that goes on down here." She strolled off. "Felix will raise a ruckus if anyone dares come near our claim. They'll be safe enough."

Grabbing the Henry, Fargo followed her to a gravel bar that jutted within jumping distance of the opposite bank. The knoll was grassy and quiet, the flat top about the size of a dinner table. From their vantage point the campfires along the creek sparkled like so many fireflies. Most of the prospectors had gone into Dew Claw for their nightly dalliance with whiskey, women, and cards, but enough remained to puncture the darkness with rowdy mirth and constant hubbub.

"The whole world seems so pretty from up here," Ella remarked. "So peaceful." She had sat well back from the edge. Her right knee was bent, her leg curving nicely from thigh to foot. "It's hard to believe all the terrible things that have happened. Today was the last straw. I'd rather die than have Mandy be hurt. I think I'm going to take Lester up on his offer." She looked at him for approval.

"Do what you think is best," Fargo said, sinking down beside her. Their arms brushed. He set the Henry on his right, then leaned back. "By tomorrow it should all be over."

Ella pursed her ruby lips. "You know who is behind all this, don't you?"

"I have a fair notion."

"And you'll refuse to tell me even if I were to drop burning embers down your britches," she said, sounding as if she might just try it.

"Well, I'd rather you stuck something else down there," Fargo bantered. Never in his wildest dreams did he think she would take him seriously. So he was doubly shocked when, without any hint of what she was going to do, she brazenly placed her hand on his leg close to his crotch.

"Have something in mind?"

Fargo turned. They were face-to-face, her warm breath fanning his cheek. Usually he could guess the motives of women when they dangled themselves before him like peaches ripe for the taking. More often than not raw lust was to blame. Sometimes they wanted to trade their charms for favors. Sometimes they were curious to learn whether his reputation in another regard was justified. But Ella mystified him. She did not seem the type to give in to lust. She did not know about his reputation as a lady's man. And the only favor he could do her was to reveal all he knew about the murders, which he had made clear he wouldn't do under any circumstances. "What are you up to?"

"Does a woman need an ulterior motive to show an interest in a man?" Ella responded.

"Most do."

Ella laughed. "Think you have us all figured out, do you? For your information I happen to like you. Isn't that reason enough?"

"What else?"

She removed her hand. "Boy, you sure know how to spoil the mood. Most men would be glad to have me throw myself at them. They'd have my clothes off so fast, my head would swim."

"I'm leaving as soon as this is finished."

"Did I ask you to marry me?" Ella asked irritably. She gazed at the tent below, sadness creeping over her beautiful features. "Truth is, Skye, I'm lonely. I need companionship, even if only for a little while. It's as simple as that." Her hand found his. "I'm acting the hussy but I don't care. Sometimes a woman just needs to be held. Is that so wrong?"

The same could be said of men. Fargo squeezed her fingers, felt her nail lightly scrape his palm. He leaned closer, their lips now a whisker's width apart. "Just so there is no misunderstanding. I don't want any hard feelings later on."

"My knight errant," Ella said, smiling. "Are you always so noble?"

"I'm honest."

"Then you're one in a million. For to be honest, as this

world goes, is to go against the grain. My pa used to say that honesty was for simpletons, but I always disagreed. Character counts. If it didn't, the human race would have wiped itself out a long time ago."

Their eyes met. In hers tiny flames were born, flames of pure passion. Ella kissed him, hard. Greedily. As if she were devouring him alive. Her velvet tongue glided over his lips and then between them to entice his. A groan escaped her when his hand rose to her right breast and covered it. Even through the fabric he felt her nipple burst erect, felt it harden. She panted and crossed and uncrossed her legs.

Fargo had plenty of time to kill. He wouldn't head to Dew Claw for two and half hours yet. Kneading her breast, he slowly pushed her down flat, then lay partly across her, thigh on thigh, their hips rubbing.

"God, I want you so much," Ella cooed when they broke for air. She removed his hat and ran her fingers through his thick hair and beard. "You're the handsomest devil I've ever laid eyes on."

"And one day you'll make some lucky man happier than any man has ever been," Fargo said, returning the compliment. She hooked her arm around his neck and pulled him down to ravish his mouth with fiery kisses too numerous to count. Where Nina had been as soft as lace, Ella was a forest fire. A raging inferno had been unleashed within her, an inferno that would not be extinguished until she experienced the release she craved.

Fargo cupped her other breast. She wriggled seductively, her knee rising between his legs to rub against his pole. It sent a ripple of excitement through him. He sucked on her upper lip, on her lower. He tweaked her nipples, first one, then the other. She rocked back and forth, moaning dreamily, adrift in a world of her own.

Fargo did not try to undress her. They were too exposed for his liking, even though there wasn't a claim within a hundred yards on that side of the creek. He contented himself with opening her shirt and sliding a hand inside. His exploring fingers worked their way under her few underthings to her marvelous globes. They were contoured like melons, as pliant as pillows, growing warm to the touch as he massaged and squeezed them to his heart's content.

"Ohhhhh," Ella whispered in his left ear, her teeth pecking lightly at his lobe. "You have no idea what you do to me."

Yes, Fargo did. He licked and kissed her neck, her throat. When his mouth reached the valley between her breasts, she opened her legs, wrapping them around his waist.

"Make me forget, Skye. At least for a little while. Please."

Her nipples were taut cherries, lush for the tasting. Fargo sucked on each in turn, rolling them with his tongue, and she arched her spine as if to push her whole body into his mouth. When he gripped both breasts and molded them into peaked hills, she gasped and heaved upward. Her nails seared his shoulders. He could feel her womanhood stroke up and down his rigid manliness through his pants. It incited him into plunging a hand into her own.

At the contact of his fingers with her nether bush, Ella stifled a cry. Fargo extended his middle finger and slid it lower, across her moist slit. Her thighs opened and closed, her hips pumped harder. She was hot enough to melt butter, and when he ever-so-slowly inserted his finger into her, she spurted. His finger was enveloped in liquid cream. Her mouth fastened on his neck as her hands plied the flesh of his upper arms.

"Ahhhh! More! More!"

Fargo was not about to stop. He pumped his finger in and out, causing Ella to rear them both off the grass. Her breaths were husky tokens of her innermost need. Her skin pulsed to his touch. As he continued to stroke she began a pelvic rhythm of her own, matching the tempo of his hand, heightening their pleasure by incredible degrees.

"I want the real thing!"

She would have to wait, Fargo thought, his mouth busy with her breasts. They were every man's ideal made real.

Their scent made him giddy, their taste was delicious enough to rival the sweetest of pastries. He lathered and licked until they glistened. All the while his finger stoked her furnace, never at rest.

"Oh! Oh! Oh!"

Ella spurted again, churning her limbs and throwing her head from side to side. It was all Fargo could do to hold onto her. When she subsided she clung to him as if afraid he would get up and leave.

Fargo tugged at her pants. They fit tight around her waist, and he had to pull and pull before they slipped over her firm buttocks and on down until they were at her knees. With a sharp wrench he freed one leg. That would have to do.

Now Ella tugged at him. Fingers flying, she undid his gunbelt. Try as she might, though, she could not get his pants below his hips without his help. When they succeeded, her hand swooped to his manhood. Fargo stiffened, his breath catching in his throat as she ran her fingers the length of his iron rod.

Ella moved her bottom nearer and rubbed him against herself. Her eyes were hooded, her lips drawn back as if she were set to take a bite out of him. "Put it in me," she requested. "I can't wait any longer."

Neither could Fargo. He aligned himself just right, then levered into her, driving himself up and in. Her inner walls fit him like a glove. Holding his body still, he relished the sensation. She smiled knowingly.

"Nina was right."

"She told you?"

"Of course. We're sisters. We share *everything*."

So the real reason came out. Grinning, Fargo held onto her hips and began a pumping motion. She matched him, the two of them as one, moving in perfect harmony. Indescribable tingles spiked his loins. Sensual sensations stimulated his spine. Their surroundings became a blur. Her breasts mashed against his chest, her nipples pinned to his skin. She gripped his chin and pulled his mouth to hers so she could feast on it. They were totally joined, Fargo adrift in a sea of carnal enjoyment. If a prospector had blundered onto them, he would not have cared. He slammed into Ella over and over and over, the slap-slap-slap of their bodies sweet music to his ears. Her head snapped back. Her hips went into a frenzy of raw abandon. It was the trigger he needed.

"Now?" she pleaded.

"Now!" he growled.

It was the explosion to end all explosions.

11

Well past midnight, and Dew Claw was lit up brighter than a Mississippi steamboat. Lanterns and torches glittered like gems. From a distance the sparkling display resembled a gleaming crown fit for a queen. Up close, though, squalor and filth shattered the illusion. Drunken, grimy prospectors trudged through bare streets, making the nightly rounds of their favorite haunts. Gaudy women in skimpy dresses paraded their physical wares on boardwalks caked with dirt. Footpads and pickpockets prowled in search of easy prey. Gunmen strutted like roosters.

Dew Claw was a simmering cauldron of violence, but the throngs reveled in the danger. It added zest to their lives, lent spice to the otherwise boring routine of their daily existence. The mining camp was a rowdy, lusty hellhole in the prime of its life, no different, and no worse, than every other mining camp Skye Fargo had visited. He rode in from the west this time, mingling with the steady stream of people pouring in and out.

As much as Fargo loved the wilderness, as much as he liked to roam the quiet places untouched by human hands, he also relished the wild and wooly nightlife places like Dew Claw had to offer. A high-stakes game of poker, a bottle of whiskey, and a willing dove on his knee, and he was as happy as could be. But tonight he was not out to enjoy himself. He had to forego tonsil varnish. He had no interest in the doves or cards. He had come for the express purpose of putting a stop to the murders, once and for all.

Logically, the Timberline Saloon was where he should start. But Fargo did not go there. He rode past the Dew Claw Mercantile. A sign out front testified it was closed. A light inside proved someone was there. Fargo reined up further down the street, dismounted, and walked back for a look-see. Moving to the side of the huge tent, he advanced in deep shadow until he heard muted voices. He drew the Arkansas toothpick and cut a small slit, careful not to shake the tent or otherwise give himself away.

The interior was dimly lit. Fargo could see merchandise piled on a table in front of him. It blocked his view. He made the slit longer but still could not see the counter. Pressing an ear to the opening, he overheard two men talking. One was Lester Cavendar. The other was unknown to him, someone with a deep, low voice.

"—did just as you told me," Cavendar was saying. "I'm not to blame if they didn't go for it. Ella told me they had to think it over. So I left. What else was I to do? Force them at gunpoint?"

"Watch your tone," the other man warned. "No, I don't blame you. I know how contrary females can be. I just hope they agree. With them out of the way, we can concentrate on what really counts."

"You'd better hope Mandy doesn't tell them who took her or there will be hell to pay." Cavendar clucked like an upset hen. "That was stupid, if you don't mind my saying so. What did you hope to prove?"

"I wanted to put a scare into them. From what you've told me, it worked."

"But the risk!" Lester declared. "And by now Rowdy Joe and Olinger are bound to have heard. They'll be fit to be tied. Especially Luke. He didn't believe sending Mundy and Lash after Fargo was such a great idea, and he'll like the latest stunt even less."

"Olinger has no cause to complain. By the time we're done, he'll be a rich man. We all will."

"Provided we live that long."

The man laughed. "You worry too much. Who's to stop us?"

"That Fargo character. You should have heard him tonight, saying how he was going to hunt us down. From the hints he dropped, I'd swear he knows it all. About us. About you. About how we're working the swindle. Everything."

"Impossible," the other man said. "How could he? Unless you've let your part slip?"

"Oh, sure. I'm dying to have my neck stretched. What do you think would happen to me if the prospectors learned I was letting you know whenever one of them brings in a high-grade sample?"

"As assayer it's your job to test ore. So what if you tell someone the results?"

"But I'm supposed to keep the information confidential." Lester swore. "Sometimes I wonder how I ever let you talk us into this. Olinger said the same thing to me just this morning. You've missed your calling, my friend. You should be a patent medicine salesman. You'd make a fortune in no time."

Fargo heard rustling, then footsteps move away.

"I'll see you in half an hour at the usual meeting place," the other said. "Bring a list of likely new prospects."

"I'll be there," Lester promised.

Whirling, Fargo ran toward the front. He had to find out if his hunch was correct. But when he reached the corner the mystery man was gone, lost amid the multitude. Then Fargo glimpsed one man who stood head and shoulders above the rest, and gave chase. The press of people hindered him. He was buffeted, shoved, forced to go slow. When he came to a junction he stopped and scoured both streets. The tall man was nowhere in sight.

Fargo slapped his leg in frustration. He had been so close! Now he must decide whether to confront Cavendar or pay the Timberline a visit. Pivoting, he retraced his steps to the mercantile. He would make Lester tell him everything. Not that there was much left to learn.

The scheme was fairly simple. Prospectors brought ore to Lester to be assayed. He noted which finds were most promising, and the information was passed on to the ring-leader. A victim was picked. Their unsuspecting quarry was lured into a card game with the gambler, a game rigged so the prospector lost his shirt. Or rather, his claim, which was signed over to one of the leaders with members of the gang as legal witnesses.

The mystery man was the brains of the outfit. Olinger's skill as a cardsharp was their means of fleecing unwary sheep. Guthrie was their curly wolf on a leash, the one who took care of problems, permanently. Lester's part was cru-cial, for not only did he assay the ore, he was also the offi-cial recorder and oversaw claim transfers.

By selecting only the richest claims, they stood to reap a bonanza. Whether they resold the claims later on or mined the sites themselves was irrelevant. Within a few short years all of them would be millionaires.

It was blatant greed, pure and simple. Olinger was already making money hand over fist as owner of the Timberline, but that was not good enough. Lester wasn't doing badly at the mercantile, what with his highly inflated prices. Yet he wasn't satisfied, either. Rowdy Joe didn't have much money but he did have the same larceny in his soul. As for the leader, he had to be the greediest of all; he had given up the most.

Fargo came to the store. The light was out, the flap had been tied. Cavendar had gone somewhere. Foiled again, he headed for the Timberline. He must discover where the meeting was to be held.

Olinger's saloon had to be the single most popular whiskey mill in all of Dew Claw. Patrons were jammed be-tween its four walls and overflowed into the street. Rather than go in the front, Fargo walked to a side entrance. A broom handle had been used to prop the door open, and peo-ple were coming and going constantly. Inside, it was a mad-house. Customers were six-deep at the bar, and the four barkeeps couldn't fill orders fast enough. The poker tables were thronged. So were the faro and roulette games. Acrid smoke hung thick overhead. The din made normal speech impossible. To be heard, a person had to shout.

Fargo moved to the left, staying close to the wall. A woman about to burst her dress sidled past and winked. A wreath of cigar smoke floated by. Attempting to spot a particular face in the crowd was like trying to find the proverbial needle in a haystack. Or it would have been, except that at the end of the bar, at the same table he had used before, sat Luke Olinger, involved in a card game. The gambler had eyes only for his hand so Fargo felt safe in moving along the wall until he was only a few yards behind Olinger's chair.

A tinny piano started to play, a woman accompanying it in a voice that would shatter eardrums were she a shade shriller. Gold hounds seated near the small stage whooped and hollered as if she were the most sensational songbird alive.

His hat pulled low, slouched over as if half drunk, Fargo scanned the saloon from under the brim. He thought he saw one or two hardcases who rode with Rowdy Joe but no sign of Guthrie himself.

Olinger was on a winning streak. He had a mountain of chips which he picked that moment to push to the middle of the table. Evidently all the other players except one had folded. A young prospector flushed with liquor stared at the pile, then matched it, using the last of his chips. Slapping his cards down, the young man crowed like a rooster. With cause. He had a full house, three jacks and two eights.

Luke Olinger said something. The prospector's smile dwindled. Spectators leaned closer to watch as the gambler slowly laid out his own hand, a card at a time. The first was the two of clubs, then a ten of hearts, a ten of diamonds, a ten of spades and a ten of clubs. Four of a kind. The pot was his.

But as the dandy began to rake the chips in, the young prospector uttered an oath and reached into a pocket. For a second Fargo thought the man was going for a gun. But it was a piece of paper the man flourished, and shoved at Luke. Olinger studied it, then nodded. Another hand was dealt.

It hit Fargo that he was seeing the scheme played out right before his eyes. The young gold hound had just bet his claim against the pot. Fargo had to stand on his toes to observe what occurred next, as more and more onlookers thronged the table.

The prospector looked at his hand, then asked for two cards. Olinger, the dealer, exchanged three. The hush in that part of the room was thick enough to cut with a knife. The young man laid his cards out flat. He was scared and it showed. "Three queens!" he declared. "Let's see you beat it!"

Luke Olinger was a master. He placed his cards down one at a time again, and as each was revealed, the prospector's face became more crestfallen. Five clubs were bared for everyone to marvel at. "I believe a straight does just that, sonny," the gambler said. "Better luck next time."

A few onlookers guffawed at the loser's expense. "That ought to teach you, Johnny," one said loudly. "Red-eye and poker don't mix."

"Dew Claw ain't no place for amateurs, that's for sure," mentioned another.

Johnny rose, in shock.

"Don't go running off, boy," Olinger said. "You have to sign your claim over to me. I'll rustle up proper witnesses."

The young prospector stepped back, the record of his claim clutched in his left hand. "This ain't right. My claim is worth ten times what was in that pot. Mr. Cavendar, the assayer, told me so himself."

"If it's that valuable you should have thought twice about wagering it," the gambler said. Reaching for his ivory-handled cane, he started to rise. "Hold on a moment and we'll go find Cavendar. Might as well make this official."

"No!" Johnny exclaimed. His hand dipped under his shirt

and flashed out holding a knife. Those nearest backed away. "I won't let you take it! I didn't realize what I was doing. All that drinking I did—"

"Is no excuse for welching on a bet," Olinger said sternly. "You lost fair and square. And you'll honor your debts, boy. Whether you want to or not."

"Like hell." Johnny looked for a sympathetic face in the crowd but there were very few. On the frontier a man's worth was judged by how well he owned up to his obligations. And to his mistakes. Johnny looked around as if searching for someone. "That other feller talked me into playing. I didn't really want to."

"You're a grown man. You make your bed, you lie in it," was Olinger's reply. "Now put away that knife before you hurt yourself. And give me the claim sheet."

"Not on your life." Johnny pivoted, scattering more patrons. "I've worked too hard and too long to make my wife proud of me. This claim means a whole new life for us. I'm keeping it, and I'll gut anyone who tries to stop me."

Defiant words, but the young man had taken only one step when Luke Olinger lunged and smashed his cane against an unprotected elbow. The knife fell to the dirt floor. Johnny, holding his arm, doubled over in agony.

"Be thankful that's all I did," the gambler said. "Now let's go." A wave of the cane, and Horner and another gunman appeared as if by magic. "Help our foolish friend, will you, boys? He needs some fresh air to clear that befuddled head of his."

No one spoke up in the young man's behalf as he was escorted out. Fargo made for the side door. For a minute he worried he would lose them. He had to fight the current, as it were, shouldering through a motley knot of revelers to the main street. But luck favored him.

The cardsharp and the forlorn prospector were moving eastward flanked by the leather slappers.

Fargo followed. At first it was easy to avoid being seen. All he had to do was blend into the crowd. But presently

Olinger turned onto a side street where there were far fewer night owls. Fargo dropped back and made it a point to shy away from patches of light. They walked and walked, the gambler twirling his cane and whistling, the young man with his head bowed in despair.

The last ragged row of tents appeared, and Fargo wondered if maybe the gambler had mounts waiting. It would take him five to ten minutes to fetch the Ovaro. By then they would be long gone.

But Fargo need not have worried. Luke Olinger ambled to a tent under a tree. Several horses were ground-hitched close by. From the open flap spilled light, bathing two cutthroats on guard outside. One puffed on a cigarette. Olinger entered, then the prospector. Horner stood in the entrance, barring escape.

Circling wide, Fargo came up on the tent from the rear. Broken limbs and twigs had to be avoided. All it would take was one loud snap to bring the gun sharks on the run. The last few feet he covered an inch at a time. Then he hunkered. Finally, he would learn who the mystery man was. The reign of terror would end.

Scornful mirth let him know Rowdy Joe Guthrie was inside. "Hellfire and damnation, boy, quit your sulking. Take it like a man. You're young. Go find another claim. Who knows? You might strike it rich twice in a row."

Guthrie and another man—Horner?—laughed. But Luke Olinger did not share in the humor. "Quit badgering him. After you've taken someone for all they're worth, you don't rub salt in the wound."

"Oh, please," Guthrie scoffed. "Since when did you get so virtuous? Why, next you'll be preaching to us to turn the other cheek."

"I might gamble for a living but I'm still a gentleman. And gentlemen have a code they live by. A way of conducting themselves." The cane tapped a hard surface. "I plied my trade on the Mississippi long before I came here, and never once did I gloat when I won."

"Maybe you should have *stayed* on the Mississippi," Rowdy Joe said. "A mining camp is no place for soft hearts or soft heads."

A commotion out front signaled the arrival of someone else. Fargo hoped it was the ringleader but it was the weasel.

"Johnny Brooks, as I live and breathe. Fancy meeting you again so soon."

A chair squeaked. "Mr. Cavendar! You're the one who told me I should go out and celebrate my new find! Look at what's happened!"

"I never meant for you to fritter your claim away at cards," Lester said.

"I knew I should leave Dew Claw," Johnny said, "but you were so insistent. And then this other jasper here, Horner, talked me into having a few drinks—" The young prospector stopped, and Fargo could have heard a pin drop. "Wait a second! I see it now! I've been hoodwinked! Played for a sucker! This whole deal was set up from the start."

Rowdy Joe snickered. "Uh-oh. We've got us a smart one on our hands. We'd better turn over a new leaf before we come to grief."

"Guthrie, you're an idiot," Luke Olinger said. "Sign a confession, why don't you?"

A shadow inside straightened. "It won't work! You hear me? I'm not signing my claim over to anyone!"

"Sit down, boy," Rowdy Joe said.

Johnny Brooks was slow of wit but not stupid. "I just realized something else. You sons of bitches must be behind all the disappearances. You've done this to others. And you make sure no one can talk by rubbing them out."

The gambler said, "Make this easy on yourself. Do as we want and it will all be over soon."

"And if I don't? What then? You'll break a few bones? Cut off a few fingers?"

"Whatever it takes," Rowdy Joe said. To the underlings outside he bellowed, "Klell! Marston! Timms! Get in here. I need you to hold our guest down while I go to work."

Fargo had not counted on this. He'd figured the gang would let the prospector leave Dew Claw to lessen suspicion, then jump him. But they were fixing to kill Brooks then and there. Which he could not allow. Rising, he rested his hand on the butt of his Colt and started around the tent.

Suddenly Fargo sensed someone off in the darkness. Spinning, he saw a horse and rider, both as black as pitch. Both were uncommonly large, the man uncommonly loud.

"Luke! Joe! It's Skye Fargo! He's behind the damn tent! Get him!"

A pistol flared in the night. Fargo answered while running. He darted toward the front as shots ripped through the canvas from within. The rider's mount reared and nickered, perhaps hurt, just as the big man fired again. Fargo reached the front corner. Klell and Marston and Timms were unlimbering six-shooters. He had no idea who was who. He shot all three, high in the chest.

Another bound carried him into the tent. Horner was turning. Fargo shoved and sent him stumbling against the table where Rowdy Joe Guthrie and Luke Olinger sat. Lester Cavendar was frozen beside a pole.

Johnny Brooks had taken advantage of the distraction to bolt for the entrance. Fargo seized him by the shirt and flung him outside. Backpedaling, he yanked on the flap as Horner heaved up onto a knee. The flap fell, screening him. Gripping Brooks, he bolted to the south.

Curses and random shots ripped from the tent. To the west hooves hammered. More riders loomed out of the gloom. Pistols cracked and hornets buzzed. Fargo fanned the hammer, expending the last round in the cylinder to give them pause.

"Who are you?" Johnny Brooks asked, huffing and puffing. "Haven't I seen you somewhere? Why are you helping me?"

Fargo was too busy reloading to reply. Bedlam had erupted at the tent. Rowdy Joe and Olinger and a limping

Horner spilled out. Rowdy Joe was livid, rasping orders, demanding a horse for himself.

"They were fixing to cheat me out of my claim and kill me," Johnny Brooks babbled on. "We have to spread the word. Get hold of Harve Barclay and some of the other bigwigs and let them know what's been going on."

"Shut up and run."

"I *am* running," Brooks replied. "I can't go any faster. But all we have to do is reach a main street and we'll be safe. They wouldn't—"

The thump-thump of a pair of slugs coring the prospector's body silenced him forever. Arms outflung, Johnny Brooks pitched to the earth like a stricken crow, bounced once, and was still.

Skye Fargo spun, crouching as another bullet whizzed above. An overeager gunman was bearing down on him at a full gallop. Flame and smoke spewed from a muzzle. Fargo responded in kind and had the satisfaction of seeing the hardcase catapult backward from the saddle. He dashed to head off the sorrel but it flew off into the murk.

"Kill him!" Rowdy Joe raged. "I want his hide or I'll have yours!"

Fargo sprinted for his life. None of Dew Claw's teeming horde were anywhere in the vicinity. Or if they were, they were wisely lying low. He looked for a mount he could borrow, for somewhere to make a stand. Members of the gang were in pursuit, both on horseback and on foot. Lead zinged by on both sides but he did not shoot back. Not yet. He could not afford to waste cartridges.

A narrow gap on his right was an alley that zigzagged among the tents and shanties. He raced along, the lusty curses of the horsemen music to his ears. They had found the alley too narrow. So either they climbed down and came after him on foot or they had to go on around. Most did the latter. Most, but not all.

Boots pounded in a flurry. A glance revealed a gunman streaking around a turn. Fargo twisted, tripped, and fell against the side of a shack as the killer's pistol boomed. The Colt was just as loud, the man's shriek as he toppled even louder. Lurching erect, Fargo resumed his flight.

Loud crashing to the left warned him of another alley, of another gunman trying to get ahead of him. To the southeast a horse whinnied. An opening to the right beckoned. He ducked into it, only to be brought up short by a darkened tent. Crouching, he strained his ears. A couple of Guthrie's men were close, very close, barreling down the alley in a headlong rush. He cocked his Colt, then thought better of the idea. The hired guns weren't the ones he wanted. They hurtled past without a sideways glance.

Fargo poked his head out and waited until they went around a bend. Then he headed back the way he had come. It was the last thing anyone would expect. At the alley mouth he stopped. He could see the tent under the tree. No one was there. The big man on the big horse was gone. Olinger and Guthrie were gone. Lester Cavendar was nowhere around. If not for the bodies, no one would know a gunfight had just taken place.

Fargo jogged southward, toward the heart of the mining camp. Fifty or sixty yards ahead people were passing back and forth in a steady flow. Odds were he could elude the gunmen once he mingled with them. He turned to check behind him, and in doing so saved his life.

From behind a shanty galloped a tall drink of water working the lever of a rifle. Four shots in swift succession rang out. Fargo felt a tug on his left sleeve but no pain. Whipping his arm straight, he drilled the gunman from forehead to crown. The man and the rifle tumbled. The horse cut to the right. So did Fargo. Leaping, he snagged the saddle horn and swung onto the saddle.

Some passers-by had heard the shots and were gathering at the junction. Let them, Fargo thought. Guthrie's gunmen would have to force their way through, giving him ample warning.

The next moment a husky shadow separated from a tent

on the left and strode into the middle of the street. Smirking, Rowdy Joe Guthrie adopted a wide stance. His pistol was in its scabbard, his arms loose at his sides. He did not say anything until Fargo reined up. "This is as far as you go, mister. Climb down."

Fargo had his revolver out. He could have shot Guthrie before the killer touched his six-shooter, but he slid off and twirled his own into its holster.

Guthrie gazed beyond him to where the rifleman had fallen. "How many does that make? I've lost count." He sighed and shook his head, then glanced at the crowd. "So much for the big man's great ideas. Keep a low profile, he said. No killing unless we had to, and no one would ever be the wiser. And that damn dandified card slick called *me* an idiot."

"Who is he?" Fargo asked. "Who's the hombre who set this whole thing up?"

"Find out for yourself," Rowdy Joe said, his hand dropping to his pistol even as he spoke.

Only a greenhorn would fall for the ruse. And Fargo was no greenhorn. Their shots were a split-second apart but his blasted first. Guthrie was smashed backward and collapsed onto his knees, then swayed like a tree in a gale. He was dead before his face and the dirt became acquainted.

Fargo climbed back on the horse. One down, three to go.

12

They could not have been more obvious if they hung out a sign that read, "Come right on in. We're waiting to kill you." Several lanterns lit up the inside of The Dew Claw Mercantile as bright as day. The front flap hung wide open.

Skye Fargo had left the horse tied to a rail down the street and walked the rest of the way. He saw two silver-haired prospectors come out of the store. They walked unsteadily, the result of too much coffin varnish. Glaring over their shoulders, they shook gnarled fists and swore mightily. Then they draped an arm over one another and came toward him. Halting, he smiled. "What happened in there? The two of you look mad enough to shoot somebody."

The men stopped. "If'n I'd had a gun, mister, I would have," the blurry-eyed grizzle-heel on the right said, slurring every word.

"Me, too," commented the other pocket hunter. "Why, the nerve of some folks!" He launched into a string of eloquent cussing.

The first man grew more incensed just thinking about it. "That uppity bastard! If a store ain't open for business, then they should have the flap tied shut. How in the hell were we supposed to know?"

"The mercantile is closed, then?" Fargo said.

The second prospector bobbed his whiskers. "Accordin' to the rude coyote who shooed us out. You should have heard how he treated us! It's gettin' so that no one respects their elders anymore."

"Treated us as if we were pond scum, he did," elaborated the first. "I'd of punched him, except he had a big ol' hog leg."

"He was one of them gunmen," the other declared. "You can always tell. They have a nasty look to 'em. Like they're itchin' to kill. When he was a sprout he probably pulled wings off butterflies for fun."

The pair moved on, muttering.

Fargo drew the Colt and verified he had six pills in the wheel. Stepping to the side of the mercantile, he went halfway to the rear. This time he cut the tent from as high up as he could reach, clear down to the ground. The toothpick went into its sheath. Parting the canvas, he quietly slipped inside. He was next to a shelf of dry goods. Two long tables, piled high with clothes, were in front of him. At the end of the table on the left was a tent support. A lantern hung from the pole.

Crouching, Fargo cat-footed to it. Rising quickly, he blew the lantern out with a single puff, then bent low again and hurried back around the table to the other side. No shots rang out, even though that section of the store had been plunged in shadow. They had to know he was there.

Or did they? Fargo peered under the tables but spotted no one. Maybe they were all at the front, he mused, watching the entrance. Maybe they hadn't noticed the lantern go out. He moved forward, exercising caution, never raising his head above the tables or venturing across an aisle without looking first.

A stack of crates had to be skirted. Fargo bore to the right, squeezing through the cramped space between the crates and the tent. And then he saw Horner.

The "rude coyote" had squatted between two high shelves, facing the flap. His Smith & Wesson was out and cocked. Never the most patient of men, he kept shifting his weight from boot to boot and tapping a finger on a shelf. He stopped when he heard the click of the Colt's hammer being thumbed back. "Well, ain't this a kick in the pants. You're one crafty son of a bitch."

"Drop the gun and you can live," Fargo whispered.

"For how long? Until the miners get their hands on me?" Horner's hat swung from side to side. "No, thanks. I'd rather be bucked out in gore than decorate a cottonwood. Choking on one's vomit is a rotten way to die."

"Your choice."

"Mind if I ask you a question before we get to it?"

"Ask."

"Are you really him? The Fargo who wiped out that Snake River outfit a while back? The outfit that was robbing pilgrims along the Oregon Trail?"

"I was there," Fargo admitted, and changed position.

"I'll be damned. My cousin was one of those you made wolf meat of. We weren't exactly close, but he was kin."

Fargo did not like how Horner had raised his voice. It struck him that the gunman was stalling. The smart thing to do would have been to shoot him in the back and be done with it. But he wasn't a back-shooter. "Enough jawing."

"My sentiments exactly," Horner said. He hurled himself to the side while spinning and bringing up the Smith & Wesson. The man had the reflexes of a cat. Against most, it would have been enough.

Fargo's shot slammed into Horner like an invisible mallet and the gunman crashed against a shelf. Clinging to stay upright, Horner brought the Smith & Wesson to bear again. Fargo shot him through the head. The killer and the contents of the lower shelves spilled to the floor.

Fargo began to pivot, to get out of there before the others pegged his position, but one of them already had. Horner's ploy had worked. Behind him the air hissed and his right arm was jarred to the bone. It went numb from elbow to fingers. The Colt plopped at his feet. He made a grab with his left hand but a polished boot stomped onto the barrel. His ribs were spiked by pain. Scrambling backward, he uncoiled.

Luke Olinger was as smug as ever. Wagging his cane, he said, "You never should have meddled. We had a good thing going until you came along." He glanced at Horner. "He went out like a man should. You'll have to grant him that."

Fargo did not grant anything.

"I should finish you, but we'll wait for Rowdy Joe. I'm sure he'd enjoy helping to carve you into little pieces for the buzzards."

"Guthrie is dead."

The gambler's grin folded. "Joe, too?" Rage seized him, rage he restrained with a visible effort. "Well then, I'll do you myself." He took a step. "Once I thought that if we let you be, you'd ride on. But I can see now I was wrong. It didn't matter what we did. You wouldn't go until every last one of us was worm food."

Fargo was shaking his arm to restore the circulation. His fingers tingled but he could barely move them. "Tell me one thing. The name of your boss."

"Why should I?" the dandy asked. "Not that I owe him any favors. I had my doubts about his scheme. But he claimed it had worked for others in California. Why not for us? In a couple of years I'll take my millions and travel to Europe. I've always wanted to visit London and Paris."

"Too bad you never will."

Olinger's face darkened. "We'll see about that." Gripping the ivory handle, he gave the cane a sharp wrench. The wooden sheath came loose, and out slid a two-foot blade much like a rapier's. Olinger deftly traced circles in the air, then discarded the sheath. "I picked this up in New Orleans several years ago. Took a few fencing lessons when I was younger. But here, let me show you what I learned."

Like a bolt of lightning, the sword cane flashed at Fargo's throat. He skipped to the rear and the gambler came after him, thrusting and swinging in smooth, practiced strokes. Fargo glimpsed cans stacked on a shelf. With a swipe of an arm he sent them flying at the dandy's legs but it didn't slow Olinger down.

"You can do better than that."

Fargo still had the toothpick, but if he bent to grab it he would be run through by cold steel. He slanted toward the entrance, then had to dodge the razor tip of the sword as the gambler darted on around to cut him off.

"No, you don't. We're ending this here." Olinger balanced on the balls of his feet, his legs well apart in a fencing posture. "Frankly, I'm looking forward to killing you. More than I've ever looked forward to killing anyone."

A large barrel on Fargo's left was filled with brooms and rakes and digging implements. Grabbing one of the handles, he yanked, and wound up with a hoe. It was not much of a weapon, but it was three times as long as the sword and the metal lip was sharp enough to inflict a serious wound. Fargo swung it in a wide arc, forcing the dandy to give ground.

Luke Olinger did not like that. He flitted in close, his cane lashing out. Fargo parried with the hoe but the sword tip skittered along the wood handle and almost impaled his arm. Jerking aside, Fargo drove the metal lip at Olinger's face. The gambler ducked, pivoted, and coiled to attack.

Just then a pistol thundered from the vicinity of the counter. A container behind Fargo shattered, spilling pickles and pickle juice. He risked a glance and saw gunsmoke shrouding the far end of the counter, but not the person who had fired.

"Lester! Damn you! Don't do that again!" Olinger yelled. "You might hit me, you simpleton!"

Cavendar didn't listen. Popping up, he squeezed off another shot from a Walker Colt, a huge, older pistol he had to hold with both hands to fire. It bucked like a Missouri mule. This time the slug missed Fargo by only a couple of inches and tore into the barrel, blowing a hole the size of a walnut in the slats.

"Stop!" Olinger fumed. The gambler was staring at the counter.

Fargo seized the moment and sprang. The hoe swished up and around. It caught Luke Olinger on the wrist as the man turned toward him, and Olinger yelped. The sword cane dropped. Fargo moved in, spearing the blunt end of the handle into the gambler's stomach. Olinger doubled over and staggered. Fargo hiked the hoe to bring it down on top of Olinger's head but another shot boomed, the slug shattering the handle and practically ripping what was left of the implement from his hands. Rotating, he threw himself behind a shelf.

There was a scuttling noise. Fargo peeked out to discover Olinger and the sword cane gone. Then he saw Cavendar taking aim and pushed backward. The bullet made a shambles of the shelf, raining bits of wood.

Flattening, Fargo let go of the broken hoe and crawled to the end of the aisle. He snaked around the next shelf, and smiled. His Colt was right where it had fallen. Scooping it up, he replaced the two spent cartridges. Movement on the other side of the tent reminded him the gambler was still a threat. He flicked the loading gate shut.

"Luke?" Cavendar hollered. "Where is he? Did I get him?"

Knees bent, Fargo crabbed past the crates, past the tables, and on past row after row of dry goods until he was at the rear of the mercantile. Always on the alert, he worked his way to the center, then crept toward the counter.

Sounds indicated Lester was doing as he had done—reloading. A box was nervously opened, a shell dropped. Cavendar whimpered in fear. "Please! Oh, please! Oh, Please! Oh, Please!"

Where was Olinger? Fargo straightened, a pile of blankets concealing him. There had been plenty of opportunity for the gambler to escape out the front. He glided around the table to the end of the counter. Glancing right and left, he rose up high enough to see over the top.

Huddled like a frightened child, Lester Cavendar was inserting a cartridge into the Walker. His finger shook so badly he couldn't hold the cartridge steady. Whining, he smacked the revolver as if it were the gun's fault, then tried again. He succeeded and smiled. Easing upward, he tilted his head, and found himself staring into the muzzle of Fargo's Colt.

"Drop the cannon."

Lester squeaked like a mouse and obeyed, the Walker landing on his foot. Grimacing, he pumped both hands into the air and cried, "Don't shoot! Please! I don't want to die!"

"You should have thought of that sooner." Fargo continued to look every which way. "When the prospectors find out what you've done, there will be no stopping them." He motioned for Cavendar to stand.

"I never hurt anyone. Honest. It was Guthrie and his boys who did the actual killing." Lester was trembling and sniffling.

"You picked the men they murdered."

"No, no, no. All I did was let them know which claims were richest in ore. They decided who to kill. Not me." Forgetting himself, Lester reached out as if to grab Fargo's arm. The sight of the Colt stopped him cold. "You've got to believe me! I've never harmed anyone. I couldn't!"

This from the man who had just tried to shoot him? Fargo thought, disgusted. "It's out of my hands."

Cavendar brightened. "No it's not! You could let me go! Just turn your back and allow me to ride on out. I swear, I'll never tell a soul what you did. It'll just be between the two of us. What do you say?"

"You're grasping at straws," Fargo said, then saw the weasel's eyes drift past his shoulder and abruptly widen. He tensed to spin but heard something that rooted him in place. A gun had been cocked.

"Don't even think it," Luke Olinger said.

Lester smiled and clapped. "Luke! Thank God! Where did you get that derringer? You've saved our bacon. Shoot him, will you?" He moved out of the way. "Hurry. I'll tell everyone we caught him stealing from my store."

Fargo was not the only one filled with disgust. Olinger came closer. "Lester, you are without a doubt the most miserable excuse for a human being I have ever met. If we didn't need you to test the ore, I'd put windows in your skull right now."

"What did I do?" Lester said, offended.

Olinger ignored him. "As for you, Fargo, I want you to set that six-gun down and turn. Pretend you're a turtle. Do it slow, with your arms up. I want you looking at me when I pull the trigger. I want to watch you die."

Fargo placed his Colt on the counter and relaxed his fingers. Lester sneered at him, confident they had him dead to rights. He began to do as the gambler wanted, but he only turned enough to see where Olinger was. Then he gripped the Colt and dropped, extending it as he fell, the front bead lining up with the gambler's expensive white shirt even as the derringer cracked. The gambler missed. Fargo didn't.

Olinger tottered, but he was far from finished. He thrust the derringer out again, firing at the selfsame instant Fargo did. Two red dots marked his frilled shirt. The dandy looked down at himself, said softly, "I'll be damned!" and died on his feet. He crashed onto a table, scattering merchandise.

Fargo levered upward, swiveling to train the Colt on Lester Cavendar. But the weasel wasn't there. Gurgles and grunts came from behind the counter. One look sufficed to show Cavendar's swindling days were over. Fargo hurried around and knelt.

Olinger's second shot had hit Lester. A hole above the sternum pumped a scarlet geyser he vainly sought to stem. Rank terror lined his features. "Help me!" he blubbered. "For God's sake, do something!"

There was nothing anyone could do. Fargo snatched a rag and placed it over the wound. "Where can I find him, Lester? Where does he hole up?"

Cavendar was fading fast. His pupils were dilated, his chest heaving. "Who?" he said weakly.

"The big man. The one who got you into this. He must have a hideout. Tell me where it is."

"Why—" Lester husked, his eyelids quivering. "Why should I?"

"He tricked you. Used you. He kept out of sight so if anyone snooped around, only Olinger and Guthrie and you would be blamed. He even staged his own death. Who would think to suspect a dead man?"

Lester's expression had grown blank, his breathing shallow. He attempted to say something but could not marshal the strength.

"Don't die on me yet, damn you." Fargo shook him. "Tell me where he is. I promise he'll join you soon. Or do you want him to get away scot-free? Would that be right, after all you've been through?"

"No," Lester croaked. His lips moved in a bubbly whisper.

Fargo had to bend low to hear what was said.

Suddenly Lester's hand clawed at his shirt, clutching the whangs. Lester rose partway, his mouth agape, struggling to say one last thing. He never got it out. Convulsing, he slumped, sobbed once, and was gone.

A crowd had collected out front. It parted as Fargo strode from the mercantile. Some pointed at the blood on his shirt and hands. Some were more disturbed by the look on his face. No one tried to stop him. No one asked what all the shooting was about. Without comment he forked the Ovaro and reined to the west.

A tap of his spurs, and Fargo was on his way to confront the man who had caused all the bloodshed, the mastermind who had brought so much suffering and heartache to so many, the human spider whose web of evil had ensnared so many. Over fifteen people had died because of him.

No more would.

Not if Fargo could help it.

Decades ago the cabin had belonged to a trapper, one of the first mountain men to brave the perils of the high country in search of prime beaver plews. It was situated in what the old-timers called a "park," a verdant basin abundant with game. A small lake shimmered nearby. In the distance Long's Peak towered to the clouds.

Fargo reined up at the edge of the clearing in which the cabin sat. Pale light played over a hide that covered the lone window. A shadow flitted back and forth across it. Tied to a sapling was a big sweaty bay, its head hung low. The animal had been ridden hard. It was significant the saddle was still on. Climbing down, Fargo pulled the Henry from the boot. He walked to a spot about eight yards out from the door. There was no need to rush in. The ringleader was getting ready to leave, raising quite a racket. Something thumped to the floor. A chair or table scraped. Pans clattered.

Then the door was yanked wide open and a big man filled the doorway. He wore a sheepskin coat and a floppy hat and had a sack thrown over a shoulder. In his left hand, held by the barrel, was a rifle. He took another step before he saw he was not alone. Astonishment turned him to stone. "You!"

"Me."

The ringleader surveyed the clearing and spied the stallion. "You came alone?"

"You sound surprised. Would you rather I brought Nina, Ella, and Mandy along? The little one knows you're alive but the older two still believe their father is dead."

"So. You've figured it out." Brian Youngblood lowered the sack to the ground. It made a loud thud. "Here I reckoned my plan was foolproof. Where did I go wrong? How did you catch on?"

Fargo did not mind saying. He had a few questions of his own. "It was little things, here and there. The morning after you came to their camp to kill me, I studied your tracks. Later on, when Ella took me to where you were supposed to have been murdered, I saw the same tracks. Coming and going. You planted that scrap of shirt. So no one would ever suspect you were involved."

"That's it? The tracks?"

"And Mandy. For a girl who had been kidnapped, she was as happy as a puppy with a new bone." Fargo paused. "She wouldn't say who took her, no matter what her sisters did. A child would only do that for someone she loved. For a parent."

Youngblood placed his right hand on his left wrist. "I took a gamble there. I wanted them to go back to Ohio. I even arranged for Lester to buy their claim. But Ella and Nina were too stubborn. So I took Mandy to show them how dangerous it was for them to stick around." He smiled. "I'm glad Mandy kept her promise not to tell."

"Let me guess. In a couple of years, once you'd milked all the best claims for every ounce of gold, you were going to show up on their doorstep. Tell them a story about being hit on the head or some such nonsense. And all of you would live happily ever after."

"That's pretty much how I figured it, yes."

"You're loco, Youngblood. You have three daughters who love you. You had everything to live for. And you've thrown it all away."

The big man's right hand drifted lower. "You don't know me. You only think you do." Anger brought him a step from the cabin. "For years I grubbed to make ends meet. I worked my tail to the bone, and for what? I could never get ahead. I even joined the rush of '49 but all I came back with were blisters."

"Thousands did the same. None of them turned to murder." Fargo recalled another point he wanted to clear up. "That's where you learned how to swindle claims, isn't it? While you were in California?"

"The Clancy outfit did it to Argonauts along Sutter's Creek. They made almost four million. Their only mistake was in not making the assayer an equal partner. He turned them in and they swung. Biggest hanging in California history." Youngblood's right hand was now on top of his left one.

Fargo nodded at the sack. "How much?"

"About thirty thousand, mostly in nuggets. Some of the

prospectors we killed had been hoarding gold on the sly. They tried to trade it for their lives."

"I'll see that your girls get all of it, after."

Brian Youngblood shifted. "Getting ahead of yourself, aren't you? I'm still alive." He gnawed on his lower lip a moment, exactly like someone else Fargo knew. "What about my youngest? What will you tell her, if it's you who walk away?"

"I won't say a word."

"But she knows I'm alive."

"You disappeared once, you'll disappear again. She'll always wonder. She'll cry a lot. But it's best if none of them know the truth. I'd rather they go through life thinking the best of you, not the worst."

"Awful decent of you," Youngblood said, only partly insincere. "Well, then. I reckon we've plumb talked ourselves out. One last thing, though. How did you know I wouldn't just give up?"

"And die of hemp fever? With your daughters watching?"

Youngblood tried one last gambit. "My sweet girls. I gather you've become fond of them. Mandy went on and on about how nice you are. So how about turning your back? For their sakes, not mine?"

Fargo sighed. If he turned around Youngblood would shoot him down in cold blood. They both knew it. He was the only person who could link Youngblood to the murders. He waited, every nerve taut. When Brian Youngblood dived to the right and leveled the Spencer, he flung himself to the left and did the same with the Henry. Youngblood banged off the first shot but the slug dug a furrow in the soil. The Henry kicked against Fargo's shoulder and he saw Youngblood recoil. Again the Spencer belched lead. Fargo centered his sights, worked the lever twice.

Brian Youngblood lay on his back, his arms and legs outstretched. Fargo slowly rose and warily approached. He kicked the Spencer well out of reach but did not lower the Henry. "Damn you for making me do this."

Sucking ragged breaths, Youngblood said, "I've been a jackass, haven't I?" A final whistling intake, and he stiffened. His limbs went slack, his Adam's apple bobbed once.

Skye Fargo gazed at the heavens. Above him seemed to float the shiny image of a beaming girl with cute freckles and pretty curls. "Damn you, Youngblood," he repeated, softly, but only the stars heard.

LOOKING FORWARD!
The following is the opening
section from the next novel in the exciting
Trailsman **series from Signet:**

THE TRAILSMAN #206

OREGON OUTRIDER

1860, the far land of Oregon
beckoned like a rainbow at
the end of the long trail of
suffering and hardship. But
to many, the rainbow was an illusion,
their only reward deceit, deception,
new suffering, and living death . . .

The three-masted barkentine had already become a two-masted vessel with the first strike of the screaming wind but it was the towering mountain of seawater that snapped the mainmast as if it were a matchstick. Ten of the crew were swept overboard as they were whipped by torn halyards, clew lines, braces, and rigging ropes that curled around each man with a deadly embrace. Left only with a foremast, the ship rolled helplessly in the raging sea. The rock-strewn shore of the Oregon coastline was lighted by the flashes of lightning that tore the black night sky open.

The towering rocks seemed to rise up with a deadly promise as they waited with malevolent patience for their victims. The ship heeled far to the port side as another massive wave struck her and when she slowly righted, the captain regained his feet on the stern deck. "The goddamn upper topsail," he screamed to the struggling figures below. "Secure the topgallant, too." Captain Juan Consalve cursed again as his battered ship shuddered under the impact of another tremendous wave. A short man with a pushed-in face, wrapped in his oilskins, he looked more like a toad than a person. His first mate, a lean, gangly figured man, pulled himself closer along the rail and the captain pointed to a crewman huddled against the rail. The sailor knelt on both knees, his head bowed, his hands held out together in prayer. "What the hell is he doing?" Captain Consalve screamed.

"He's praying. He won't move," the mate shouted back.

"Kick his ass," Juan Consalve roared back. "Get him to the foremast."

"He won't go. He's asking forgiveness. He says the storm is punishment for what we are doing," the mate said. The captain saw two crewmen halt and stare at the kneeling figure. Pulling a heavy Bentley percussion five-shot pistol from under his oilskins, he steadied himself against the pitch of the ship and fired off two shots. The praying crewman fell over dead and was immediately swept along the deck by a breaking wave. The other two crewmen tore their eyes away from the sight and ran to the foremast. Juan Consalve pocketed the pistol in satisfaction. He couldn't have the crew getting ideas about praying for salvation. He wanted only their muscles and bodies working to keep the ship afloat. They'd have time for praying if they were swept overboard.

The thought had just left the captain's mind when another terrible gust of wind sent his vessel heeling to port again. As he clung to the stern rail he saw a mountain of seawater join the wind to tear away all the sails on the foremast except the upper and lower topgallants. Trailing broken yardarms, shredded canvas, ropes, blocks, and assorted shrouds, the sails washed out into the churning sea. With only two sails left on the remaining mast, the ship was propelled helplessly by the raging wind. "Lower the boats," Juan Consalve shouted to his first mate.

"In these seas?" the mate questioned.

The captain pointed to the rocks. "You want to stay with the ship?" he asked. "It's hitting the rocks for sure. We've a chance with the boats." The mate nodded and started to hurry away. "Wait," the captain called. "Go down to the hold. Bring up the girl . . . the Peking merchant's daughter. She'll bring enough to buy us a new ship."

"What about the others?"

"Leave them."

"Tied up?"

"You want them fighting us for the boats?" Consalve asked. The mate nodded and fought his way along the rolling deck, well aware the vessel carried only two lifeboats. The captain grimaced as he saw the spray-drenched rocks just ahead of the vessel. They'd do better riding the surface of the churning sea in the two lifeboats, he knew. Unlike the ship, the lifeboats had a chance to skirt their way between the rocks. But he was sweating inside his oilskins, fear gripping his short, squat form, his lips drawn back as he saw the ship being hurled directly at a huge rock. The mate reappeared dragging a slender figure in a gray, one-piece dress. "Lower the boats," the captain shouted as he swung down to the main deck and felt the ship gather speed atop a towering wave.

The young woman pushed jet-black, wet hair from her face. "There are two hundred people tied below decks. They'll drown when we hit the rocks," she said.

"Most of them. Some might make it. We'll get any who do," Juan Consalve said.

The young woman struck out, trying to rake her nails across his pushed-in face. "Monster," she screamed. But he caught her arm and flung her to the deck.

The mate picked her up and pulled her to where the two lifeboats were being lowered and threw her into the first one as if she were a sack of potatoes. Captain Juan Consalve fought through a drenching blast of seawater to reach the lifeboat, which was already filled with crew members. The black-haired young woman lay on the floor of the lifeboat as he knelt beside her, barking orders at the six crewmen manning the oars. The boat was lowered and immediately swept up atop a churning wave. "Row for the rocks," the captain shouted. "I'll tell you when to turn." Clutching the gunwale of the lifeboat with both hands, the captain peered through the wind and water, a lightning flash showing him the two rocks dead ahead. He waited, lips drawn back, as the sea swept the boat in a sudden rush toward the rocks. "Now, now. Turn, goddammit, turn," he shouted. The crewmen pulled hard on the oars, digging paddles into the top of churning waves, and with excruciating slowness, the boat began to turn.

There was a space behind the first towering rock, the captain had already seen, and now the lifeboat came abreast of it. With a little luck, they could slip through, he saw, grabbing the oar of the nearest crewman and pulling it along with him. The sea cooperated, lifting the boat and sending it swirling through the space between the rocks, and continuing to send it racing toward a smaller, lower line of rocks. They'd hit and be tossed into the swirling sea, the captain saw, but not with the force that they'd avoided. Juan Consalve firmly believed in the triumph of evil over good. He had spent a lifetime working to prove that.

The big man with the lake-blue eyes sat quietly inside the cave, warm and dry. He had seen the storm coming a little before dusk, and had sent his Ovaro into a fast trot as he rode a few thousand yards behind the Oregon coastline. He had seen these fierce storms sweep the coast. He knew the total fury of their terrible power and he sent the horse into a canter as he searched for a place of safety. He found the cave, well within sight of the coast, only an hour before the storm struck. Tall enough to accommodate the pinto, he rode in, unsaddled the horse, and stood at the mouth of the cave to see the sea already pounding the rocks of the shore. The wind and the rain quickly followed, becoming a howling chorus as night fell. He turned back and found enough pieces of dry wood to make a small fire as the wind and the rain grew louder.

Grateful he had found the cave, it was part of the area called the Devil's Elbow. Appropriately enough, he thought, a rugged, thickly forested part of the Oregon coast he had only ridden once before. He munched on a strip of cold beef jerky as he listened to the howl of the storm grow louder. Rising, he stood at the mouth of the cave and peered out into the night. A tremendous flash of lightning turned night into day for a second, long enough to let him see what was left of a ship heading for the rocks. Another lightning flash showed the vessel had but one mast left and the wind and driving seas were hurling it straight at the rocks.

Skye Fargo's lips drew back in a grimace. Those still aboard the ship had little chance for survival. They'd pay the price for hugging the Oregon coastline to save a few precious weeks. They all tried that now. But it wasn't always so, he remembered, before gold was discovered in California in '49. From there, gold fever quickly spread into Oregon. Not many ships sailed the Oregon coastline before that event—a few American hide droghers, wood vessels from Australia, frozen meat ships from New Zealand, and some small South American traders. But after the discovery of gold, a stream of British merchantmen, French barkentines, Portuguese schooners, and American slippers sailed the Oregon coast. The wreck in the darkness in front of him was just the latest of many and as he watched, another flash of lightning let him see the vessel smash into the rocks. It shuddered, then came apart in all directions.

The dark flooded back again and the wind screamed but he could hear the shattering of wood. Then, through the howl of the wind, he heard another sound, the scream of human voices somehow rising above the din of the storm. He squinted through the blackness, listening, and he could still hear the cries. Waiting, he peered hard, straining his eyes, but the lightning flashes grew less frequent. He could only catch the sounds but he couldn't see the bodies tossed into the air by the tremendous waves. He could not see how, tied together, they were sent whirling through the air as if part of some grotesque daisy chain. Finally, the sounds faded and he retreated into the cave where he lay down and catnapped till the silence woke him.

The storm had ended and Fargo rose to his feet, stepped to the entrance of the cave, and peered out toward the shore where the moon had come out to linger at the edge of the horizon. The night neared an end, the moonlight a pale glow on the rocks and the broken remains of the ship. The first tint of dawn touched the distant sky soon afterward and he waited, watching until the new day began to spread itself across the scene. The seas still raged but the rest of the scene held an eerie peacefulness under the new sun, only the turbulent seas and the shattered ship's hulk any evidence that the storm had struck. Suddenly Fargo found himself leaning forward as he caught a glimpse of movement along the shoreline. He picked out figures along the sand and the rocks. They moved back and forth, plainly searching. Survivors searching for their comrades, a scene made of hope and drawn-in poignancy.

Turning, Fargo went into the cave, saddled the Ovaro, and slowly rode into the open. He'd help them search. It was the least he could do. He let the pinto pick its way along the still-slippery terrain toward the shore, the horse stepping carefully among the rocks, tough shore brush, wide patches of yellow-orange agoseris, reminiscent of dandelion but much hardier, and growths of thick-leafed, fernlike plants. Beyond lay the wet, hard-packed sand of the beach and beyond that, the rocks where the ship had been impaled. Fargo's eyes went to figures coming onto the rocks this side of the beach and he counted at least seven figures searching, then spied another group of five tied together with a length of rope. Two more figures stood with them.

The pinto skirted a flat rock when the horse halted and reared back. "Easy," Fargo murmured, his eyes going to the patch of wide-leafed shore growth that lay still flattened by the force of the rain that had deluged them. He urged the pinto forward but once again the horse refused and backed away. Long ago, Fargo had learned to trust that instinctive wisdom, the special sixth sense animals possessed beyond anything humans could muster. Drawing the Colt at his hip, he dismounted. As he pushed the thick-leafed brush back with his foot, he felt his eyes widen as he looked down at the slender figure that lay beneath the brush. Jet-black hair, cut short, finely formed features, and eyes black and almond-shaped, she stared up at him from a face of delicate Oriental beauty. Chinese, he guessed, from the fine formation of her high cheekbones. But it was the expression in her jet eyes that held him, a terrible pleading made of fear, desperation, and a fierce anger that glittered through everything else. He frowned at her wet form, her body curled up into a fetal position. She made no sound but her eyes pleaded for help, crying out for him not to reveal she was there.

Fargo let the thick fronds fall back into place and the slender figure disappeared from sight under them. The frown dug hard into his brow as he led the pinto forward, skirting the spot, as questions whirled through his mind. Had the girl been aboard the ship? If so, why was she hiding? Survivors didn't hide. Or was she something other than a survivor?

Was she on her own, no part of the wrecked ship? The question asked itself again. Why was she hiding, so clearly fearful of being discovered? The frown was still digging into his brow as he reached the first line of rocks before the wide beach. A short, squat but powerfully built figure wearing a captain's cap and uniform, barked orders to the seven men combing the rocks. Fargo's eyes went to the five figures that were tied together and saw each wore wrist irons. The two men with them carried rifles, he noted. And he noted something else. The five shackled figures were all Chinese.

A strange uneasiness began to creep through him as he moved closer and the man in the captain's uniform turned, came toward him. Fargo took in a pushed-in face, small eyes, and thick lips. "You from the ship?" Fargo asked.

"*Sim.* Captain Juan Consalve," the man said, his accent very Portuguese.

"Portuguese trader?" Fargo questioned.

"*Sim.*" The man nodded.

"Came down to see if I could help. Didn't think there'd be anyone left alive," Fargo said.

"A few of us survived," the captain said.

Fargo's eyes went to the five shackled figures. "Why the wrist irons?" he queried.

"Prisoners, from your jails. We were taking them back when the storm hit," Consalve said. Fargo's glance stayed on the five men. All were plainly Chinese and none wore prison uniforms, though that didn't mean a lot in itself. Yet the fact clung inside him.

"All prisoners and all Chinese," Fargo remarked casually. "Kind of strange." His casual tone belied the sharpness in his lake-blue eyes. The captain paused, plainly searching for an answer.

"They were all part of a gang," he said, finally.

Fargo nodded, smiling inwardly. The captain had the smarts to think quickly, his answer both plausible and reasonable, yet stretching probability. Fargo couldn't dismiss it but a warning pushed at him and the image of a fearful young Chinese girl hiding under the wet fronds flashed through his mind. Something was not quite in order at these scenes of a shattered ship and drowned passengers. Did the terrible storm hide evil inside tragedy? The thought lay in his mind as he moved the pinto a step backward. "I'll search some on my own. Might just find some more survivors," Fargo said.

"Whatever help you can give us," the captain said. "Call us if you find anyone."

"Sure thing," Fargo agreed and sent the Ovaro at a slow walk along the wet rocks, his eyes sweeping the terrain, the barnacle-covered rocks, the flat sand, and the creviced coastal ridges. As the sun warmed the earth, it brought out the brilliant beauty in pods of starfish and glinted on barely submerged beds of anemone. But no figures came before his sweeping gaze and he started to close a wide circle that would bring him back to where he'd seen the hidden girl. He saw Juan Consalve and six of his crew near the spot, searching with their heads lowered. The captain pointed to places in the rocks. They had picked up tracks, footprints that had been pressed into wet sand and leaves and were still visible. Suddenly, as a hound that had suddenly caught a scent, Consalve moved quickly to the exact spot where the girl lay hidden. Fargo moved the Ovaro forward as the captain bent over and ripped the heavy fronds aside. There was a lean man with him, and with a triumphant shout, the captain pulled the girl out of her hiding place.

He slapped her in the face, knocked her to the ground, and pulled her to her feet again as Fargo came up. "That's enough," Fargo barked. The captain stopped and glared up at him. "Funny way to treat survivors," Fargo said.

"I know what I do," the captain growled. "You can go your way, mister."

"She a prisoner, too?" Fargo asked, edging the horse forward.

"Not for you to worry about. Move on, senor," the man said. The young woman's eyes met Fargo's and he saw hurt and betrayal in the jet orbs, which shot a quick glance at the captain and the six men with him. All looked back glowering and he took note of the pistols they carried stuck in their belts. All cumbersome, slow-firing European handguns, he noted. None of the men looked as though they'd be fast on the draw, he wagered silently. The advantage would be all his in an opening exchange, Fargo knew, just as he knew exactly what he had to do to send them scattering and give himself the precious seconds he'd need. He didn't want killing if he could avoid it, not with only unanswered questions and more shadow than substance in hand. Drawing a deep breath, he pulled the Colt from the holster at his hip at the same time he sent the Ovaro leaping forward.

He aimed his first shot. The captain clutched his shoulder as he cursed in pain and dropped his hold of the girl. Fargo whirled and fired a volley of shots that had the six crewmen diving for safety. Leaning from the saddle, he scooped the girl up into the saddle in front of him. Pressing her head down, he sent the Ovaro racing away, their shots following. The ground offered no cover and they had enough guns to lay down a solid barrage when they stopped shooting wildly. He sent the Ovaro charging toward the cave as more shots hurtled after him. The horse slipped twice on the still-wet underfooting, but it recovered each time and reached the cave as the next volley of shots fell short. After Fargo moved the horse into the cave, he loosened his hold on the girl and she slid from the saddle.

Fargo dismounted, the girl's eyes on him as he brushed past her to peer from the mouth of the cave. In the distance, Juan Consalve was gathering more of his crew together as one wrapped a cloth around his shoulder. Fargo felt the girl come alongside him. Still-wet, jet-black hair clinging to her head, the one-piece dress clinging to her slender body, she nonetheless stood very straight beside him, smallish, high breasts perfect on her shape. "Don't figure you'll understand me but I didn't turn you in back there," Fargo said.

"I know," she said softly in English which had hardly the trace of an accent. "That was plain when you took me from them."

"You speak English." He frowned, surprise flooding through him.

"Yes. I am Mei Ling," she said, her voice softly sensuous.

"Fargo, Skye Fargo," he said, still wrestling with his surprise.

Mei Ling's eyes went to Consalve and the others. "What will they do?" she asked.

"Attack, sooner or later," Fargo said. A shiver coursed through her slender form. He took a blanket from his saddlebag. "Take those wet clothes off," he said and stepped to the edge of the cave. Mei Ling came beside him moments later, almost lost in the blanket wrapped around her. He took the wet dress and spread it on a stone in the sun just outside the cave. "It ought to dry out in an hour," he said.

"Will they wait?" she asked.

"They're in no hurry. They figure all they have to do is come get us or wait for us to try and run," Fargo said.

"Are they right?" she asked.

"I don't figure to let them be," he said, lowering himself to the floor of the cave. She followed and sat beside him with the blanket demurely wrapped around her. "You've a lot of questions to answer," Fargo said brusquely. "You were on the ship, I take it." She nodded. "How'd you live through the wreck?" he queried.

"The crew left the ship before it hit the rocks. The captain had me taken along. When the lifeboat made it between rocks, I was on it. But I saw a chance and ran away on-shore," Mei Ling said. "That's where you found me hiding."

"Suppose you start from the beginning, tell me every-thing."

"Everything?"

"About the captain, the ship, about you," Fargo said. "Start with where you learned English."

"In Peking, in special school for languages. My father is a silk merchant in Peking. I was well educated," she said.

"What were you doing sailing on a Portuguese trader?" Fargo asked.

"Coming here to America. Over two hundred of us," Mei Ling said. "Only they turned us into prisoners, all of us."

Fargo wanted to question her more but his keen ears heard the sound from outside. Turning, he saw two of the crewmen creeping forward, one on each side of the approach to the cave. "You can tell me the rest later," he said. "We've some visitors that need discouraging."